D1133074

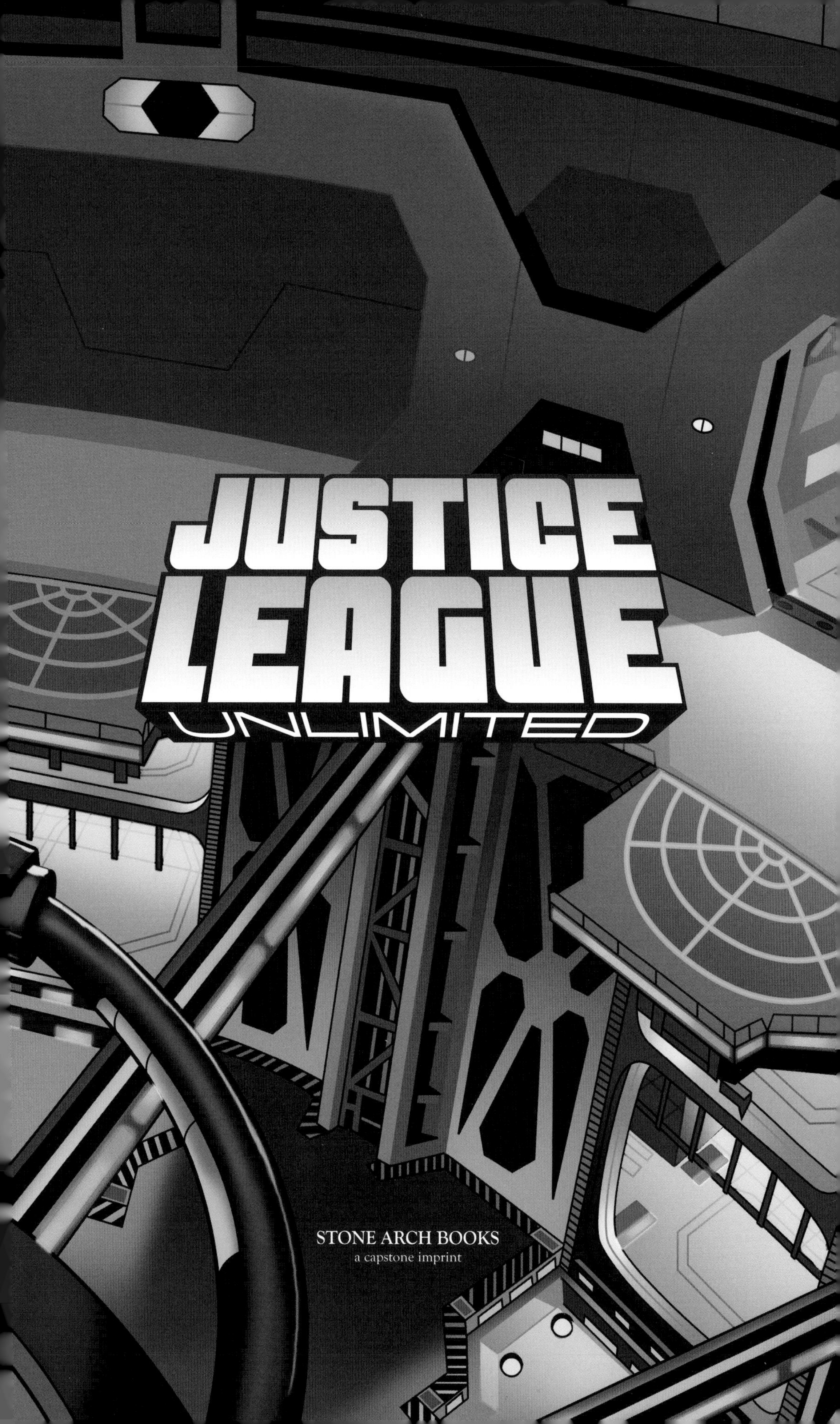

JUSTICE LEAGUE UNLIMITED

STONE ARCH BOOKS
a capstone imprint

STONE ARCH BOOKS™

Published in 2013
A Capstone Imprint
1710 Roe Crest Drive
North Mankato, MN 56003
www.capstonepub.com

Originally published by DC Comics in the U.S. in single
magazine form as Justice League Unlimited #4.
Copyright © 2013 DC Comics. All Rights Reserved.

DC Comics
1700 Broadway, New York, NY 10019
A Warner Bros. Entertainment Company

No part of this publication may be reproduced in
whole or in part, or stored in a retrieval system, or
transmitted in any form or by any means, electronic,
mechanical, photocopying, recording, or otherwise,
without written permission.

Printed and bound in the United States of America.
082017   010719R

Cataloging-in-Publication Data is available at the
Library of Congress website:
ISBN: 978-1-4342-4716-2 (library binding)

Summary: When a young boy on the planet Rann wonders
why his world doesn't have its own heroes, Adam Strange
must show him what it means to be a hero!

STONE ARCH BOOKS

Ashley C. Andersen Zantop *Publisher*
Michael Dahl *Editorial Director*
Donald Lemke *Editor*
Heather Kindseth *Creative Director*
Bob Lentz *Designer*
Kathy McColley *Production Specialist*

DC COMICS

Tom Palmer Jr. *Original U.S. Editor*

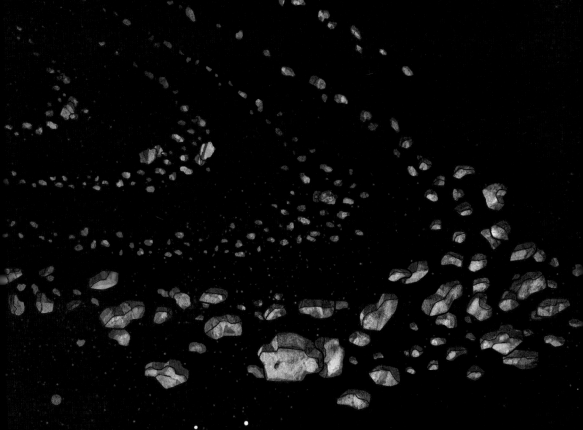

JUSTICE LEAGUE UNLIMITED

LOCAL HERO

Adam Beechen................................... writer
Carlo Barberi ....penciller
Walden Wong...................................... inker
Heroic Age .... colorist
Nick J. Napolitano ....letterer

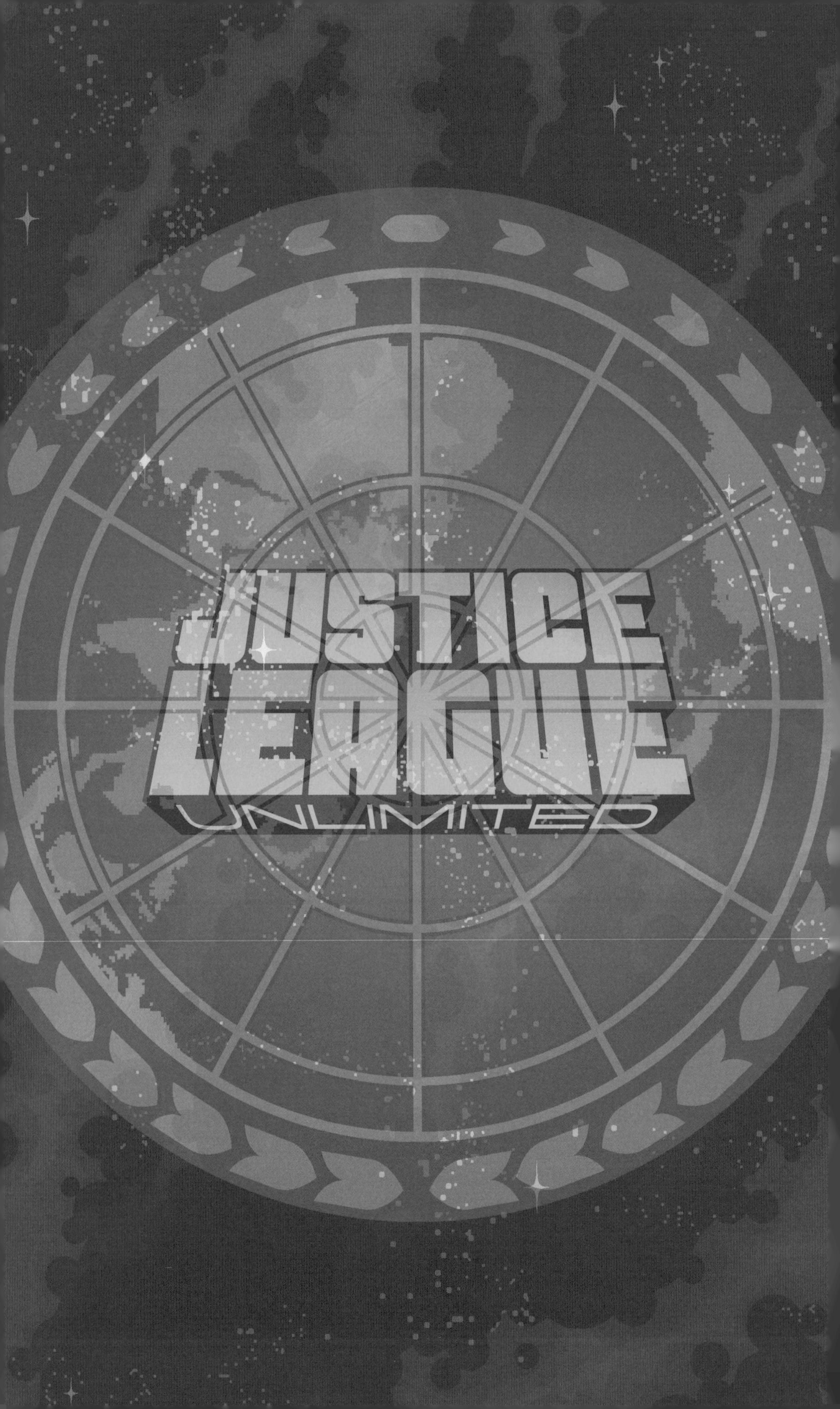
JUSTICE LEAGUE
UNLIMITED

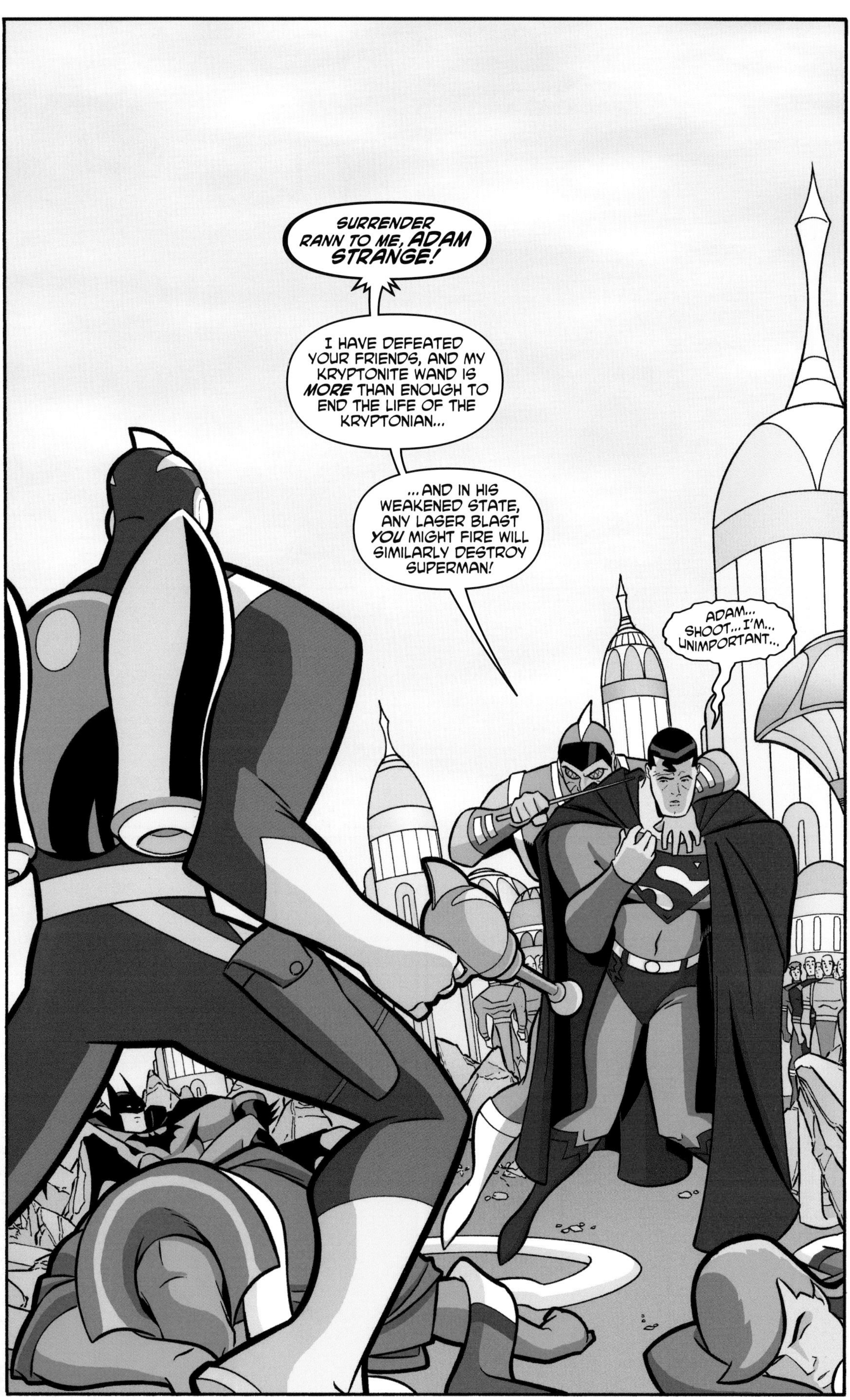
SURRENDER RANN TO ME, ADAM STRANGE!
I HAVE DEFEATED YOUR FRIENDS, AND MY KRYPTONITE WAND IS MORE THAN ENOUGH TO END THE LIFE OF THE KRYPTONIAN...
...AND IN HIS WEAKENED STATE, ANY LASER BLAST YOU MIGHT FIRE WILL SIMILARLY DESTROY SUPERMAN!
ADAM... SHOOT... I'M... UNIMPORTANT...

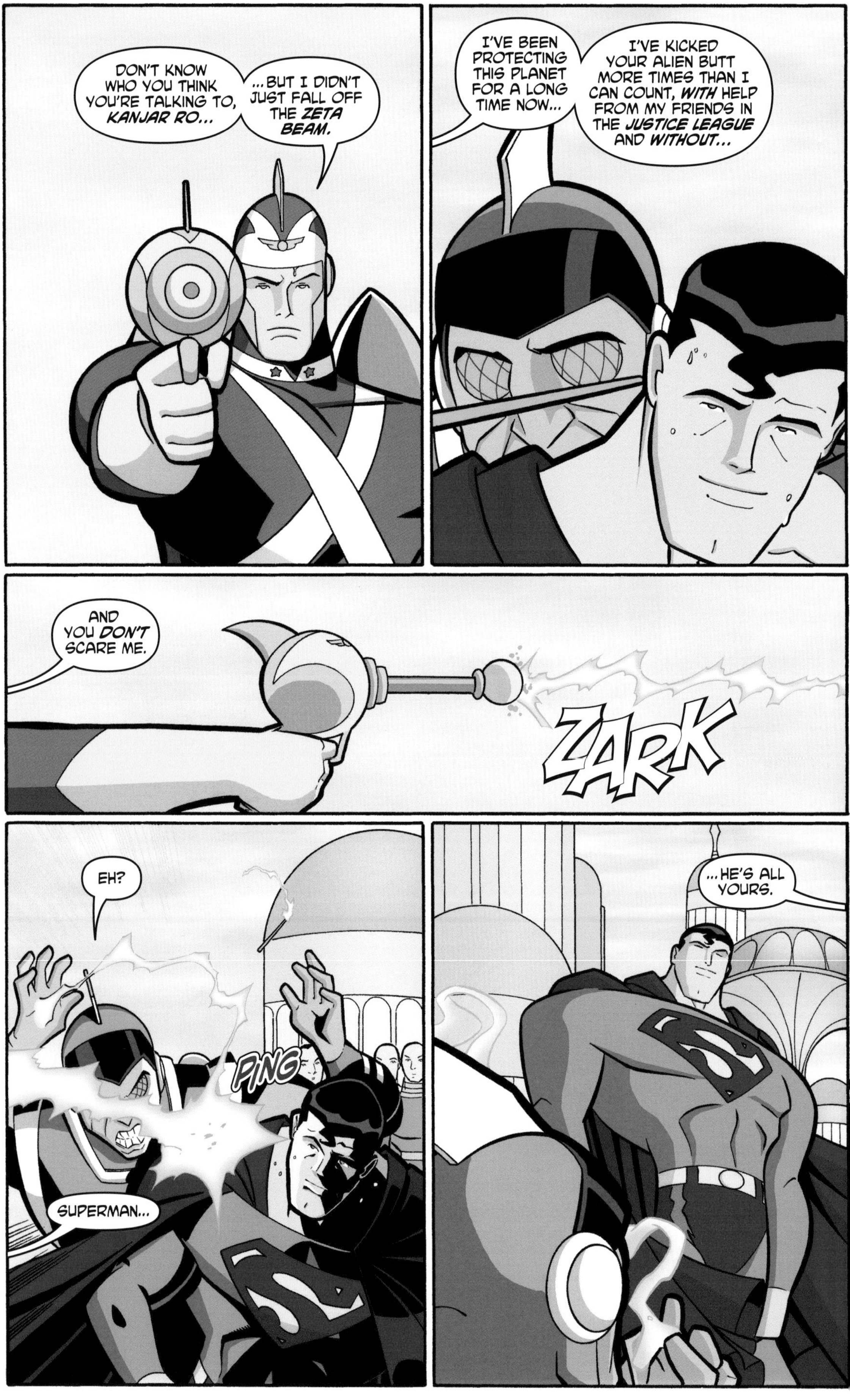
DON'T KNOW WHO YOU THINK YOU'RE TALKING TO, KANJAR RO...
...BUT I DIDN'T JUST FALL OFF THE ZETA BEAM.
I'VE BEEN PROTECTING THIS PLANET FOR A LONG TIME NOW...
I'VE KICKED YOUR ALIEN BUTT MORE TIMES THAN I CAN COUNT, WITH HELP FROM MY FRIENDS IN THE JUSTICE LEAGUE AND WITHOUT...
AND YOU DON'T SCARE ME.
ZARK
EH?
PING
SUPERMAN...
...HE'S ALL YOURS.

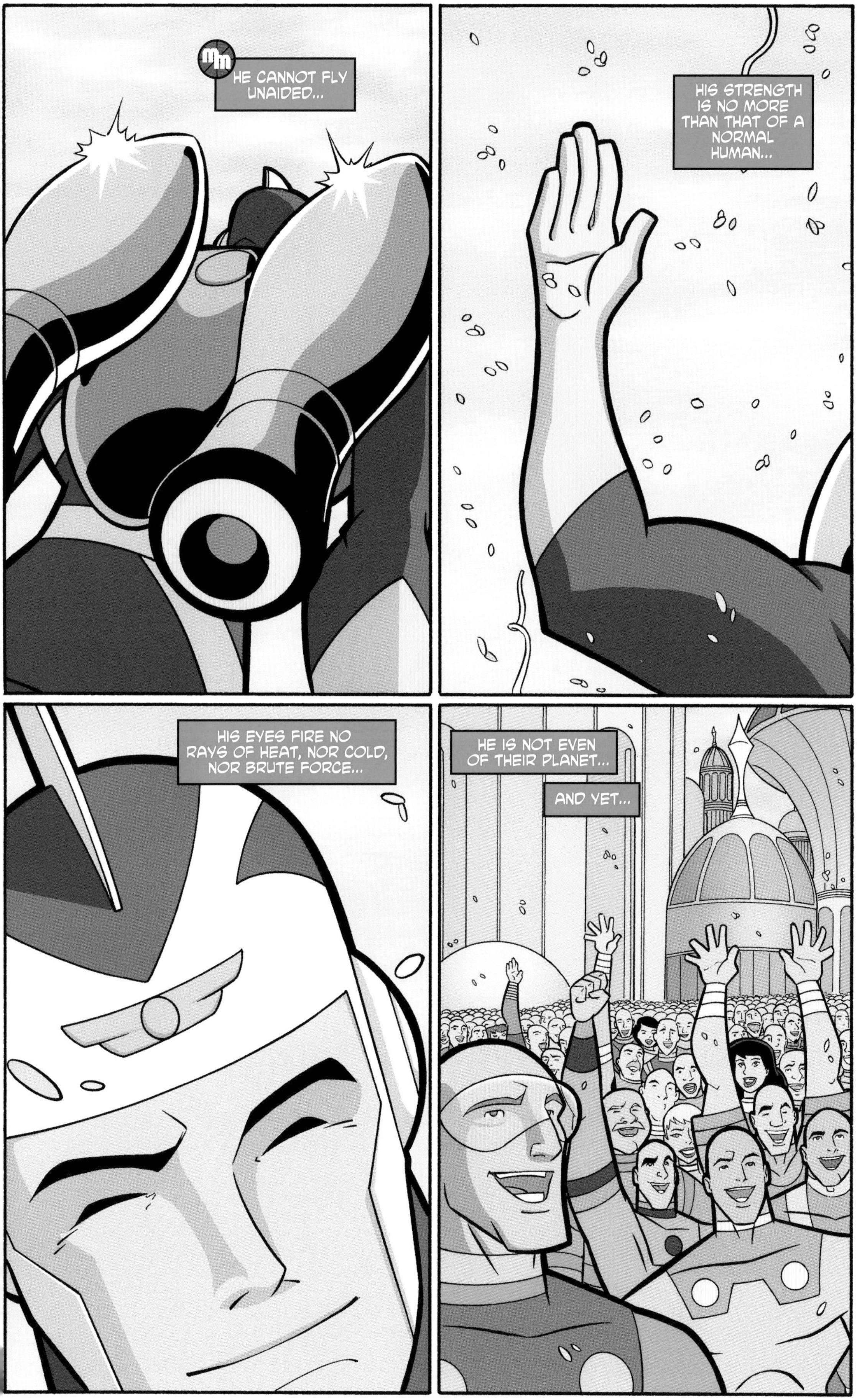
HE CANNOT FLY UNAIDED...
HIS STRENGTH IS NO MORE THAN THAT OF A NORMAL HUMAN...
HIS EYES FIRE NO RAYS OF HEAT, NOR COLD, NOR BRUTE FORCE...
HE IS NOT EVEN OF THEIR PLANET...
AND YET...

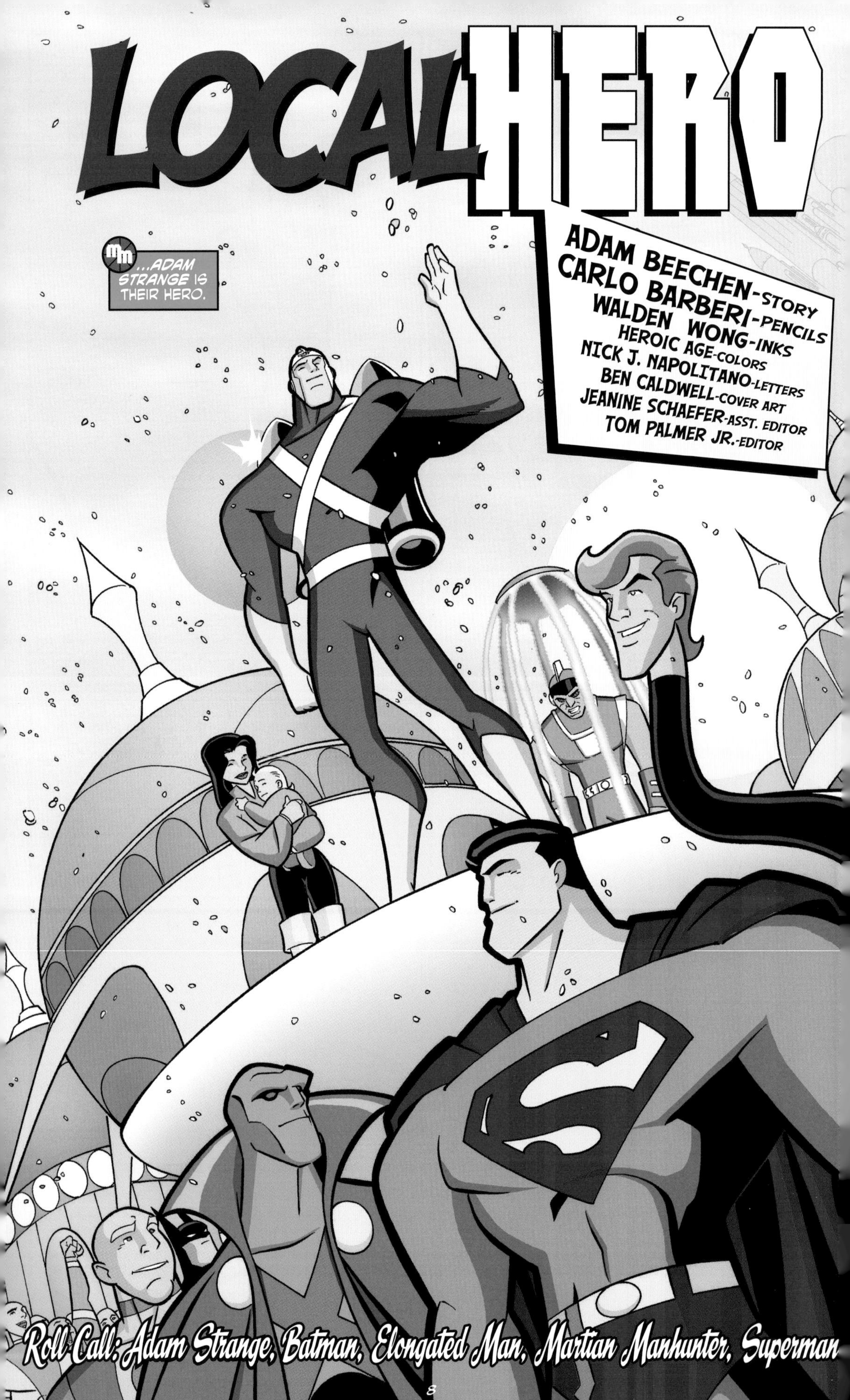
LOCAL HERO
...ADAM STRANGE IS THEIR HERO.
ADAM BEECHEN-STORY
CARLO BARBERI-PENCILS
WALDEN WONG-INKS
HEROIC AGE-COLORS
NICK J. NAPOLITANO-LETTERS
BEN CALDWELL-COVER ART
JEANINE SCHAEFER-ASST. EDITOR
TOM PALMER JR.-EDITOR
Roll Call: Adam Strange, Batman, Elongated Man, Martian Manhunter, Superman

I HAVE SEEN THE PEOPLE OF EARTH TREAT *SUPERMAN* THIS WAY...

...BUT HE IS *SUPERMAN.*

SARDATH... THE CITIZENS OF RANN DO THIS *OFTEN?*

EVERY TIME HE SAVES THE PLANET, YES...

FROM THE MOMENT HE WAS ACCIDENTALLY BROUGHT HERE BY MY EXPERIMENTAL *ZETA BEAM,* ADAM STRANGE HAS BEEN OUR *PROTECTOR.*

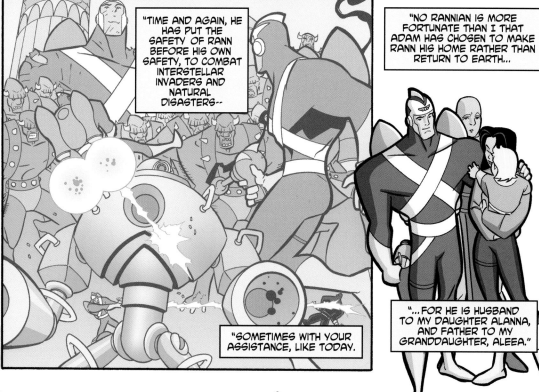

"TIME AND AGAIN, HE HAS PUT THE SAFETY OF RANN BEFORE HIS OWN SAFETY, TO COMBAT INTERSTELLAR INVADERS AND NATURAL DISASTERS--

"SOMETIMES WITH YOUR ASSISTANCE, LIKE TODAY.

"NO RANNIAN IS MORE FORTUNATE THAN I THAT ADAM HAS CHOSEN TO MAKE RANN HIS HOME RATHER THAN RETURN TO EARTH...

"...FOR HE IS HUSBAND TO MY DAUGHTER ALANNA, AND FATHER TO MY GRANDDAUGHTER, ALEEA."

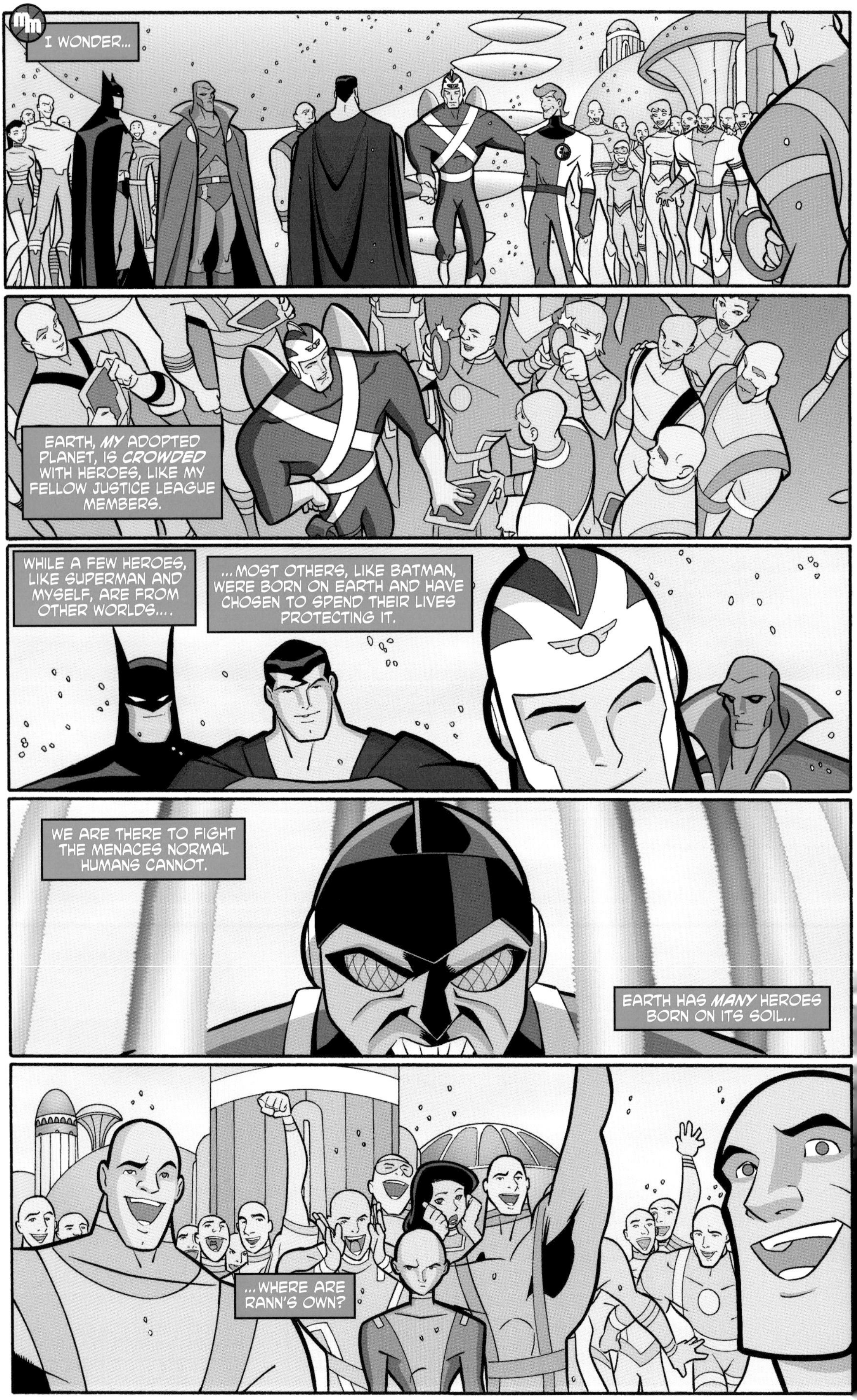
I WONDER...
EARTH, MY ADOPTED PLANET, IS CROWDED WITH HEROES, LIKE MY FELLOW JUSTICE LEAGUE MEMBERS.
WHILE A FEW HEROES, LIKE SUPERMAN AND MYSELF, ARE FROM OTHER WORLDS....
...MOST OTHERS, LIKE BATMAN, WERE BORN ON EARTH AND HAVE CHOSEN TO SPEND THEIR LIVES PROTECTING IT.
WE ARE THERE TO FIGHT THE MENACES NORMAL HUMANS CANNOT.
EARTH HAS MANY HEROES BORN ON ITS SOIL...
...WHERE ARE RANN'S OWN?

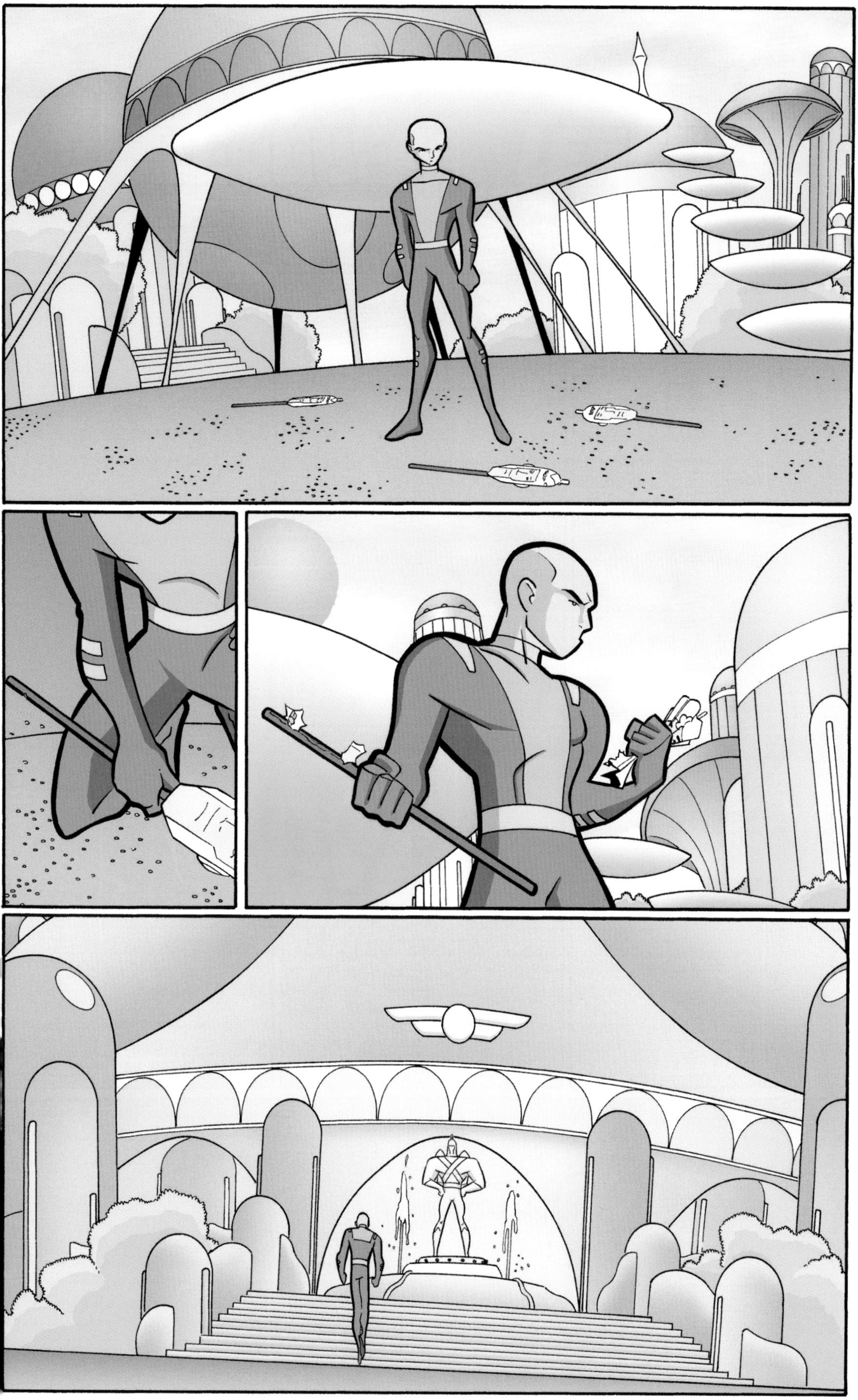

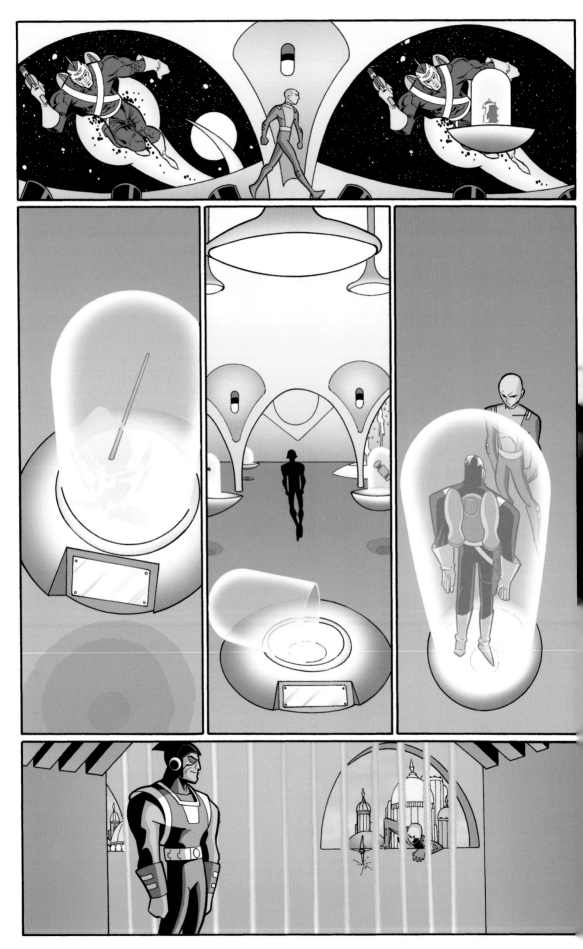

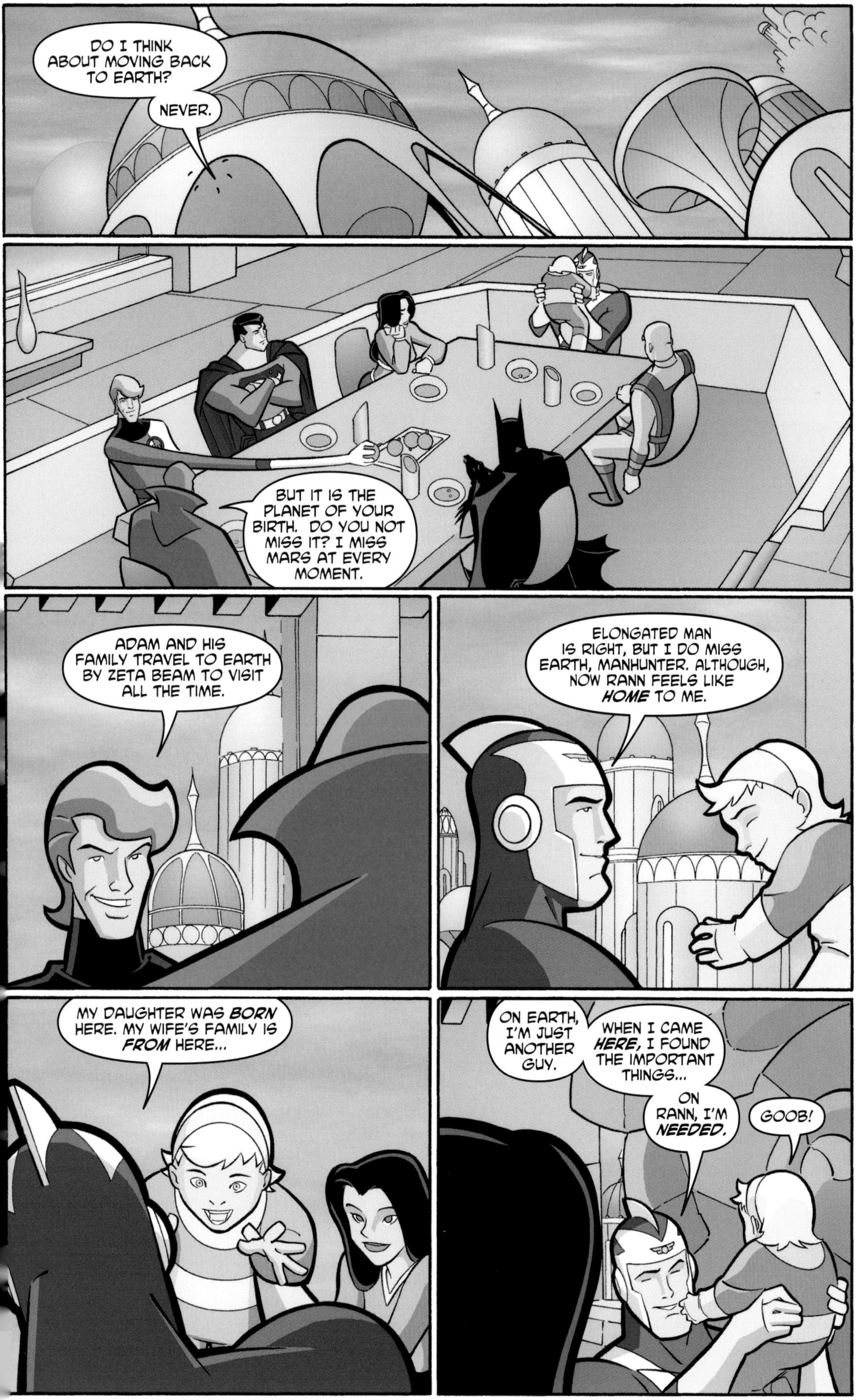
DO I THINK ABOUT MOVING BACK TO EARTH?
NEVER.
BUT IT IS THE PLANET OF YOUR BIRTH. DO YOU NOT MISS IT? I MISS MARS AT EVERY MOMENT.
ADAM AND HIS FAMILY TRAVEL TO EARTH BY ZETA BEAM TO VISIT ALL THE TIME.
ELONGATED MAN IS RIGHT, BUT I DO MISS EARTH, MANHUNTER. ALTHOUGH, NOW RANN FEELS LIKE HOME TO ME.
MY DAUGHTER WAS BORN HERE. MY WIFE'S FAMILY IS FROM HERE...
ON EARTH, I'M JUST ANOTHER GUY.
WHEN I CAME HERE, I FOUND THE IMPORTANT THINGS...
ON RANN, I'M NEEDED.
GOOB!

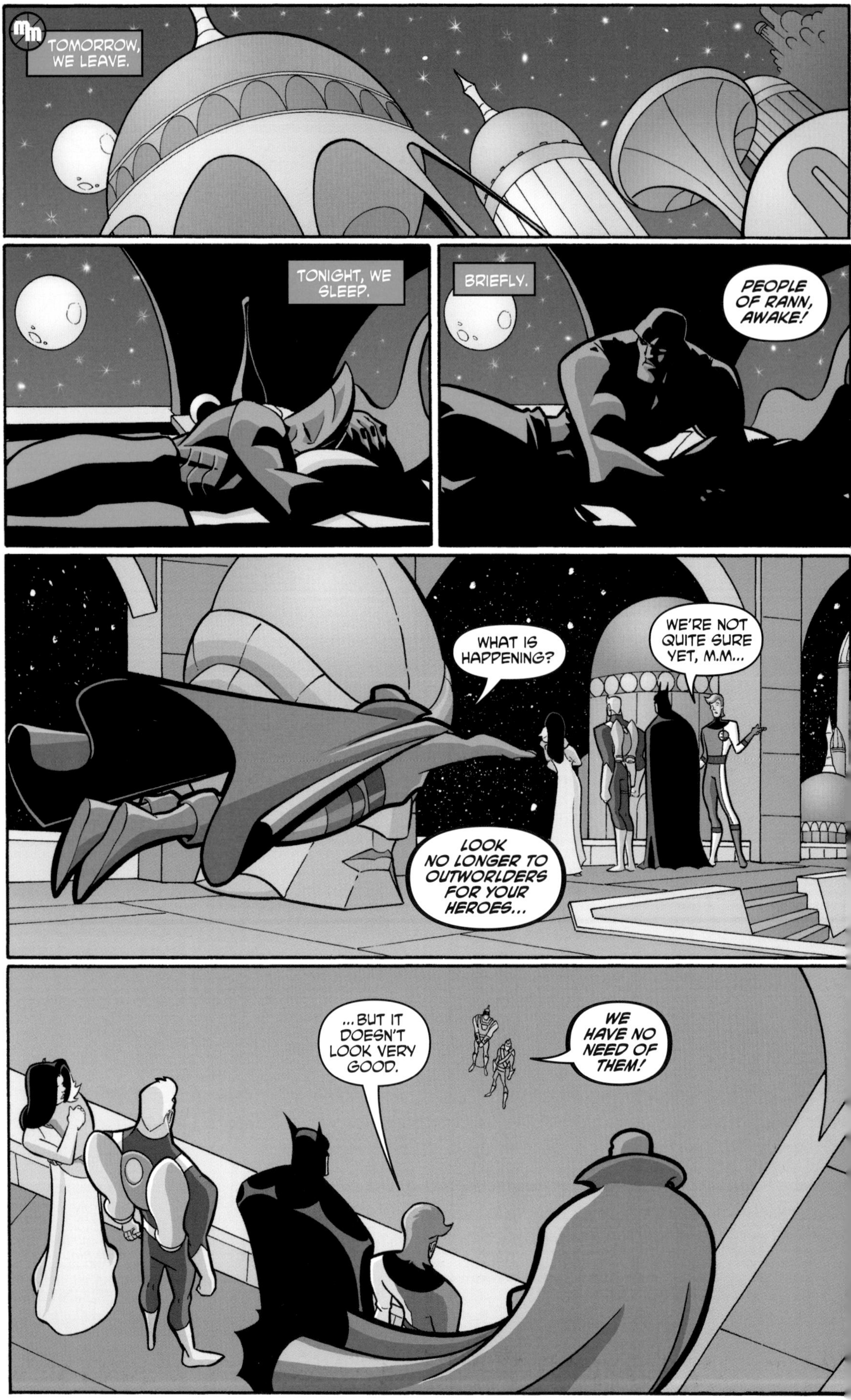
TOMORROW, WE LEAVE.
TONIGHT, WE SLEEP.
BRIEFLY.
PEOPLE OF RANN, AWAKE!
WHAT IS HAPPENING?
WE'RE NOT QUITE SURE YET, M.M...
LOOK NO LONGER TO OUTWORLDERS FOR YOUR HEROES...
...BUT IT DOESN'T LOOK VERY GOOD.
WE HAVE NO NEED OF THEM!

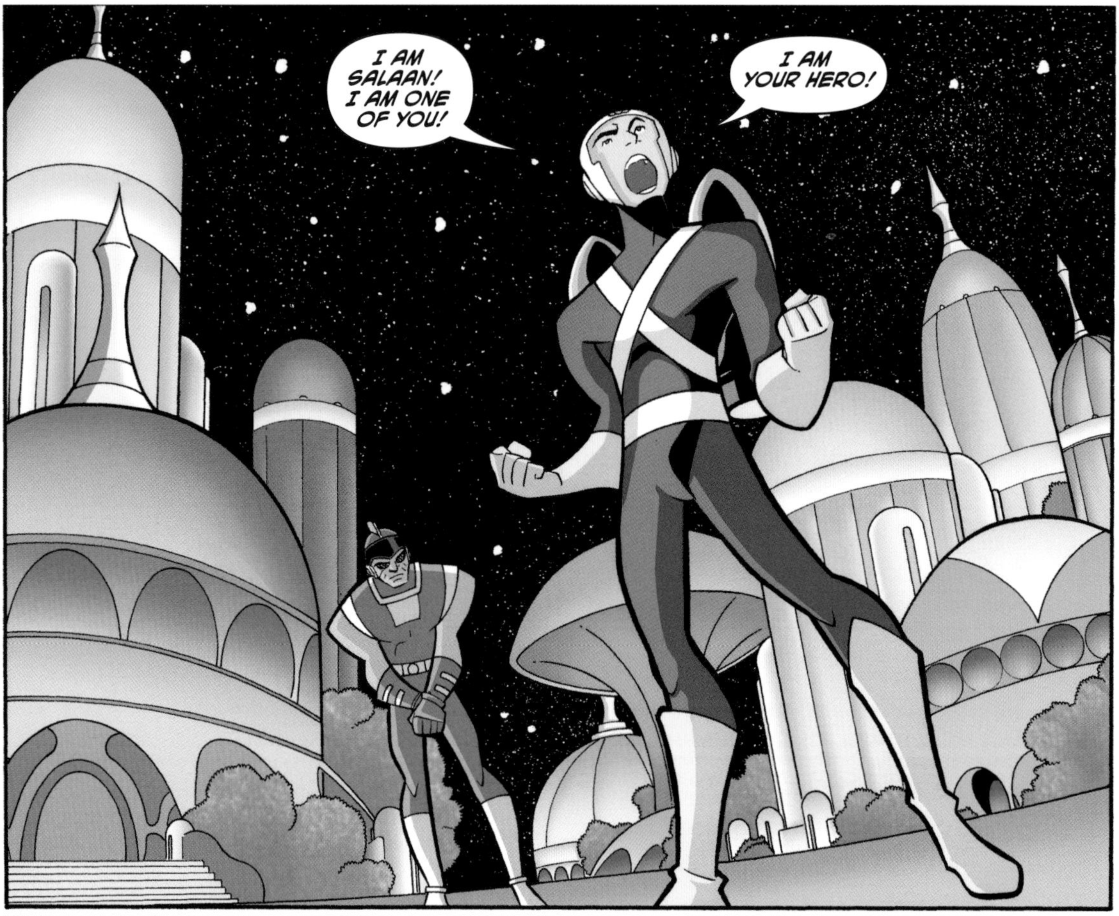
I AM SALAAN! I AM ONE OF YOU!
I AM YOUR HERO!

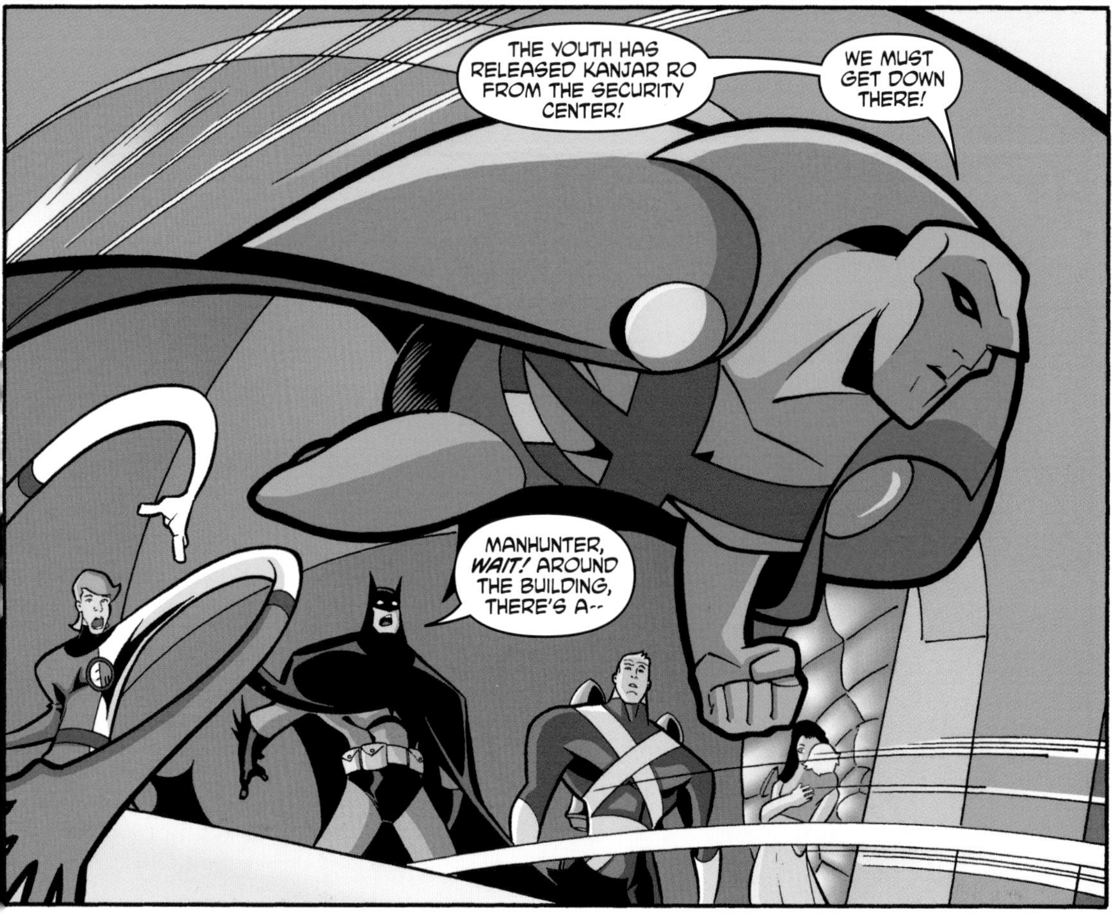
THE YOUTH HAS RELEASED KANJAR RO FROM THE SECURITY CENTER!
WE MUST GET DOWN THERE!
MANHUNTER, *WAIT!* AROUND THE BUILDING, THERE'S A--

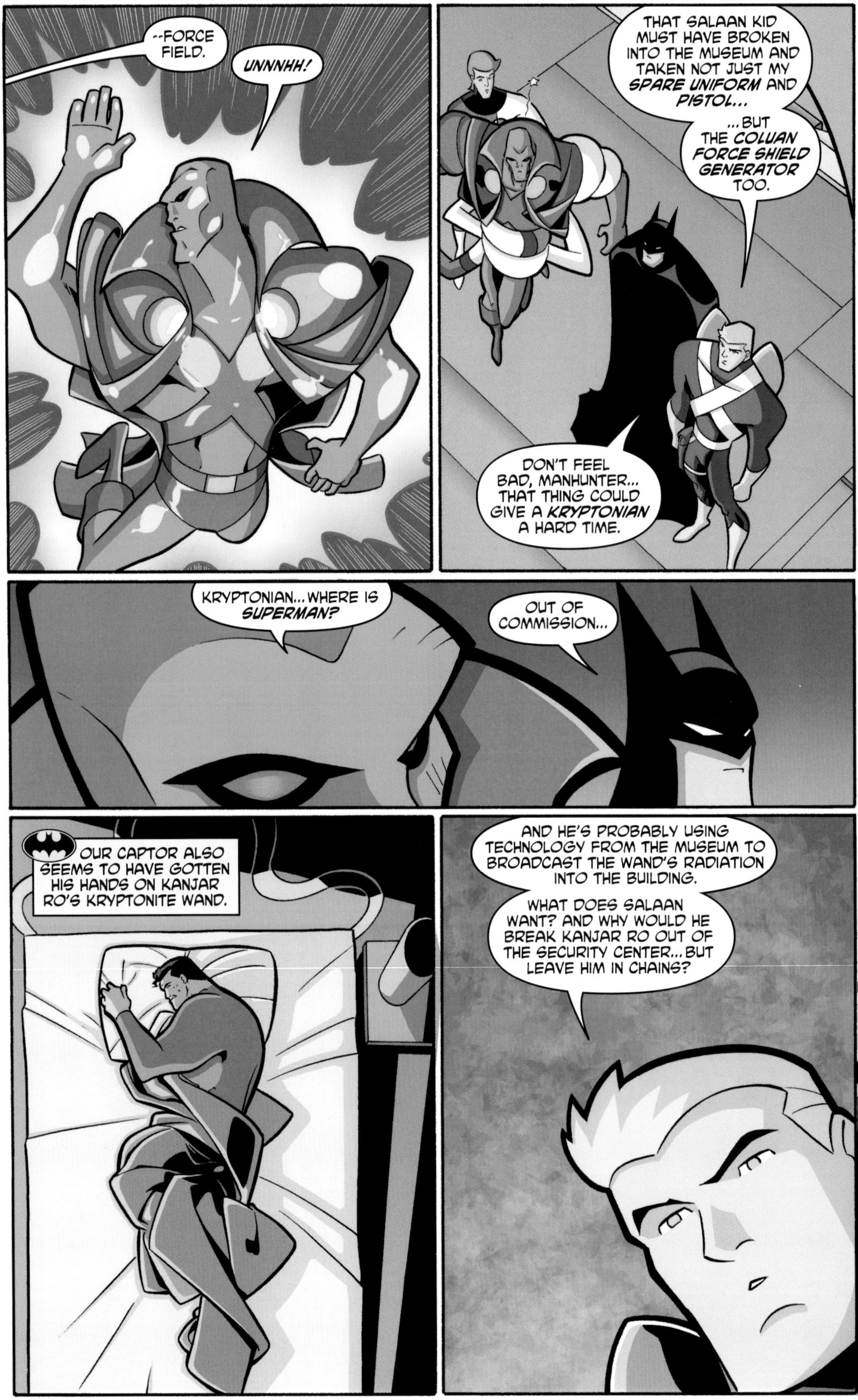
--FORCE FIELD.
UNNNHH!
THAT SALAAN KID MUST HAVE BROKEN INTO THE MUSEUM AND TAKEN NOT JUST MY SPARE UNIFORM AND PISTOL...
...BUT THE COLUAN FORCE SHIELD GENERATOR TOO.
DON'T FEEL BAD, MANHUNTER... THAT THING COULD GIVE A KRYPTONIAN A HARD TIME.
KRYPTONIAN... WHERE IS SUPERMAN?
OUT OF COMMISSION...
OUR CAPTOR ALSO SEEMS TO HAVE GOTTEN HIS HANDS ON KANJAR RO'S KRYPTONITE WAND.
AND HE'S PROBABLY USING TECHNOLOGY FROM THE MUSEUM TO BROADCAST THE WAND'S RADIATION INTO THE BUILDING.
WHAT DOES SALAAN WANT? AND WHY WOULD HE BREAK KANJAR RO OUT OF THE SECURITY CENTER... BUT LEAVE HIM IN CHAINS?

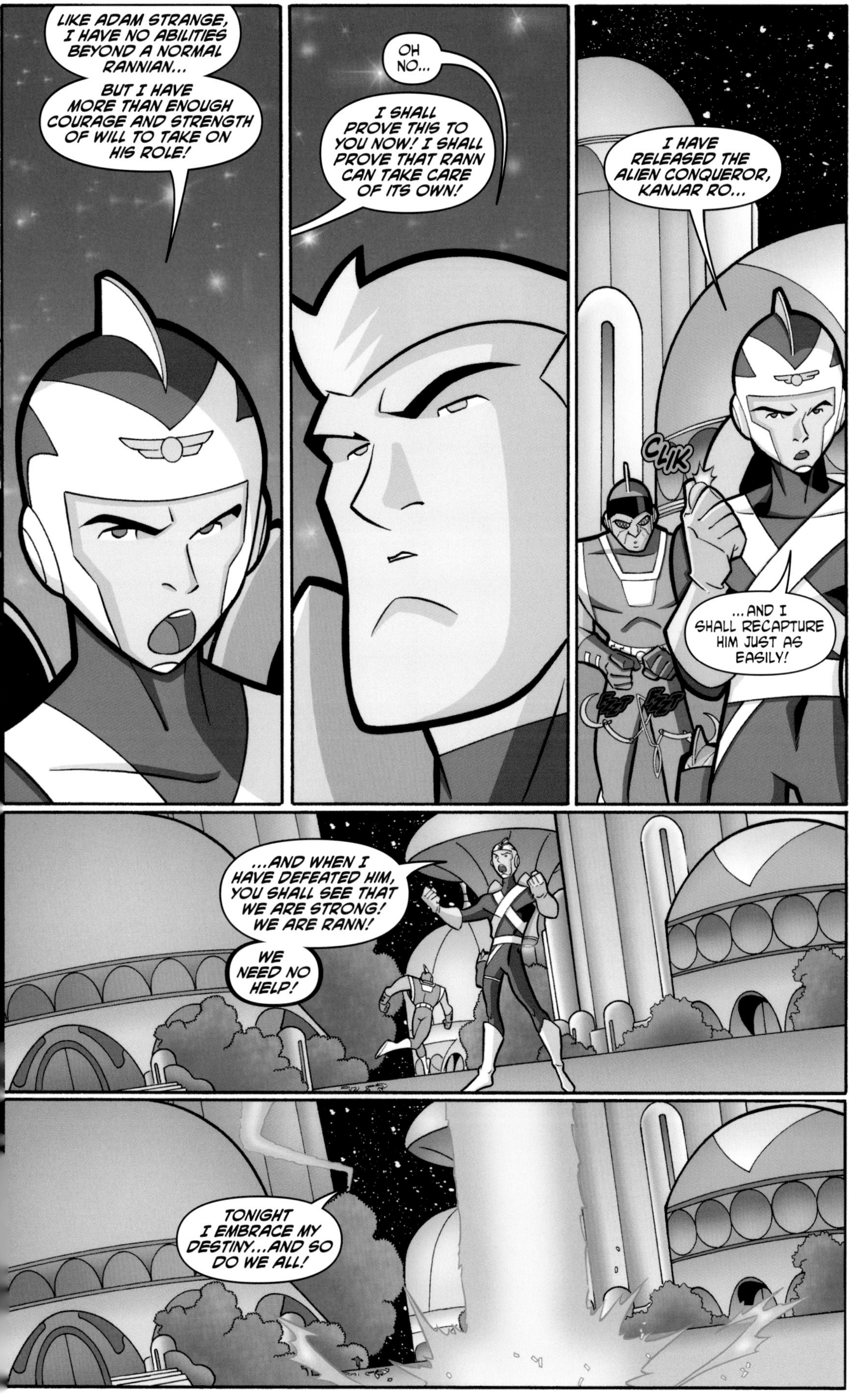
LIKE ADAM STRANGE, I HAVE NO ABILITIES BEYOND A NORMAL RANNIAN...
BUT I HAVE MORE THAN ENOUGH COURAGE AND STRENGTH OF WILL TO TAKE ON HIS ROLE!
OH NO...
I SHALL PROVE THIS TO YOU NOW! I SHALL PROVE THAT RANN CAN TAKE CARE OF ITS OWN!
I HAVE RELEASED THE ALIEN CONQUEROR, KANJAR RO...
CLIK
...AND I SHALL RECAPTURE HIM JUST AS EASILY!
...AND WHEN I HAVE DEFEATED HIM, YOU SHALL SEE THAT WE ARE STRONG! WE ARE RANN!
WE NEED NO HELP!
TONIGHT I EMBRACE MY DESTINY...AND SO DO WE ALL!

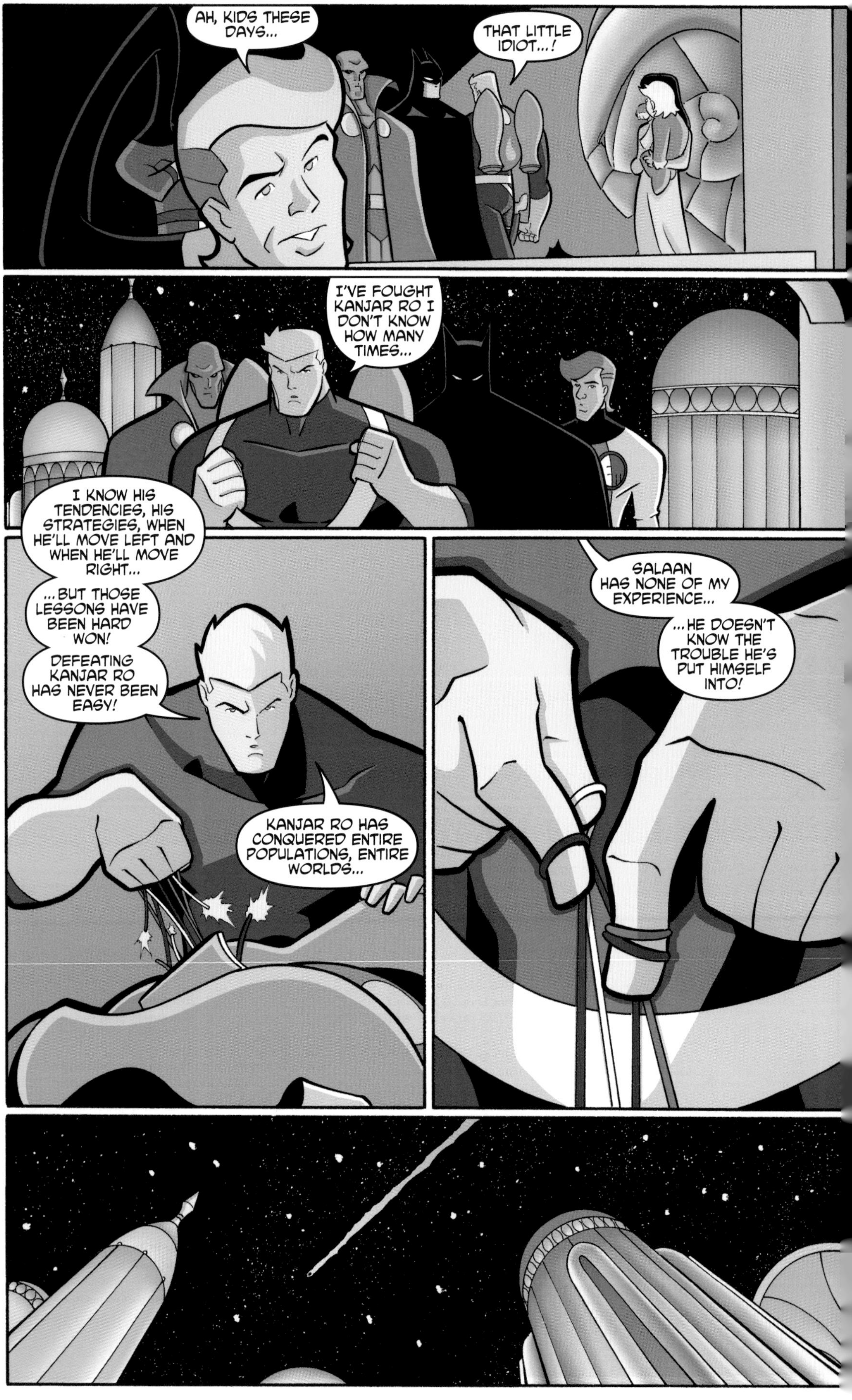
AH, KIDS THESE DAYS...
THAT LITTLE IDIOT...!
I'VE FOUGHT KANJAR RO I DON'T KNOW HOW MANY TIMES...
I KNOW HIS TENDENCIES, HIS STRATEGIES, WHEN HE'LL MOVE LEFT AND WHEN HE'LL MOVE RIGHT...
...BUT THOSE LESSONS HAVE BEEN HARD WON!
DEFEATING KANJAR RO HAS NEVER BEEN EASY!
KANJAR RO HAS CONQUERED ENTIRE POPULATIONS, ENTIRE WORLDS...
SALAAN HAS NONE OF MY EXPERIENCE...
...HE DOESN'T KNOW THE TROUBLE HE'S PUT HIMSELF INTO!

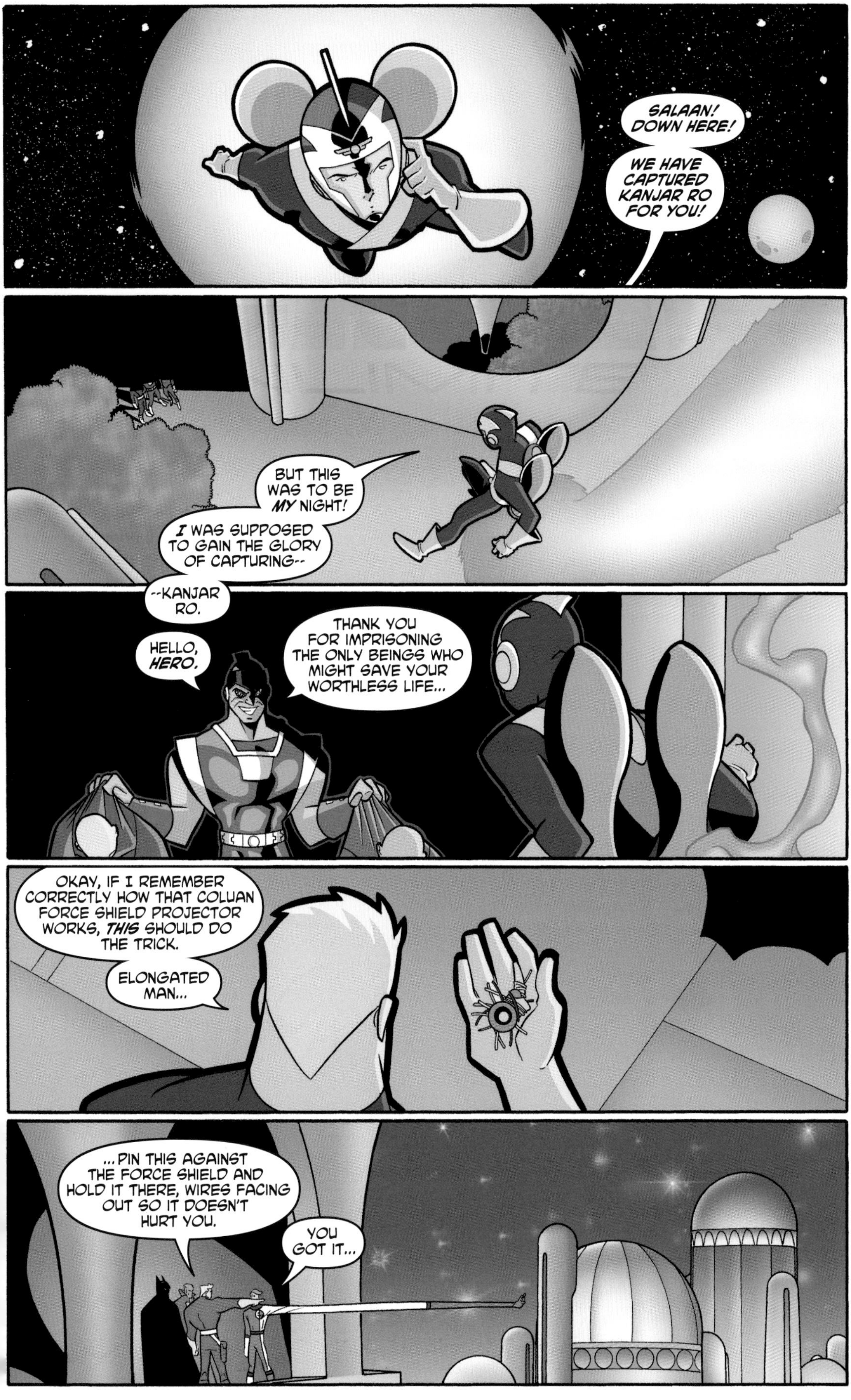
SALAAN! DOWN HERE!
WE HAVE CAPTURED KANJAR RO FOR YOU!
BUT THIS WAS TO BE MY NIGHT!
I WAS SUPPOSED TO GAIN THE GLORY OF CAPTURING--
--KANJAR RO.
HELLO, HERO.
THANK YOU FOR IMPRISONING THE ONLY BEINGS WHO MIGHT SAVE YOUR WORTHLESS LIFE...
OKAY, IF I REMEMBER CORRECTLY HOW THAT COLUAN FORCE SHIELD PROJECTOR WORKS, THIS SHOULD DO THE TRICK.
ELONGATED MAN...
...PIN THIS AGAINST THE FORCE SHIELD AND HOLD IT THERE, WIRES FACING OUT SO IT DOESN'T HURT YOU.
YOU GOT IT...

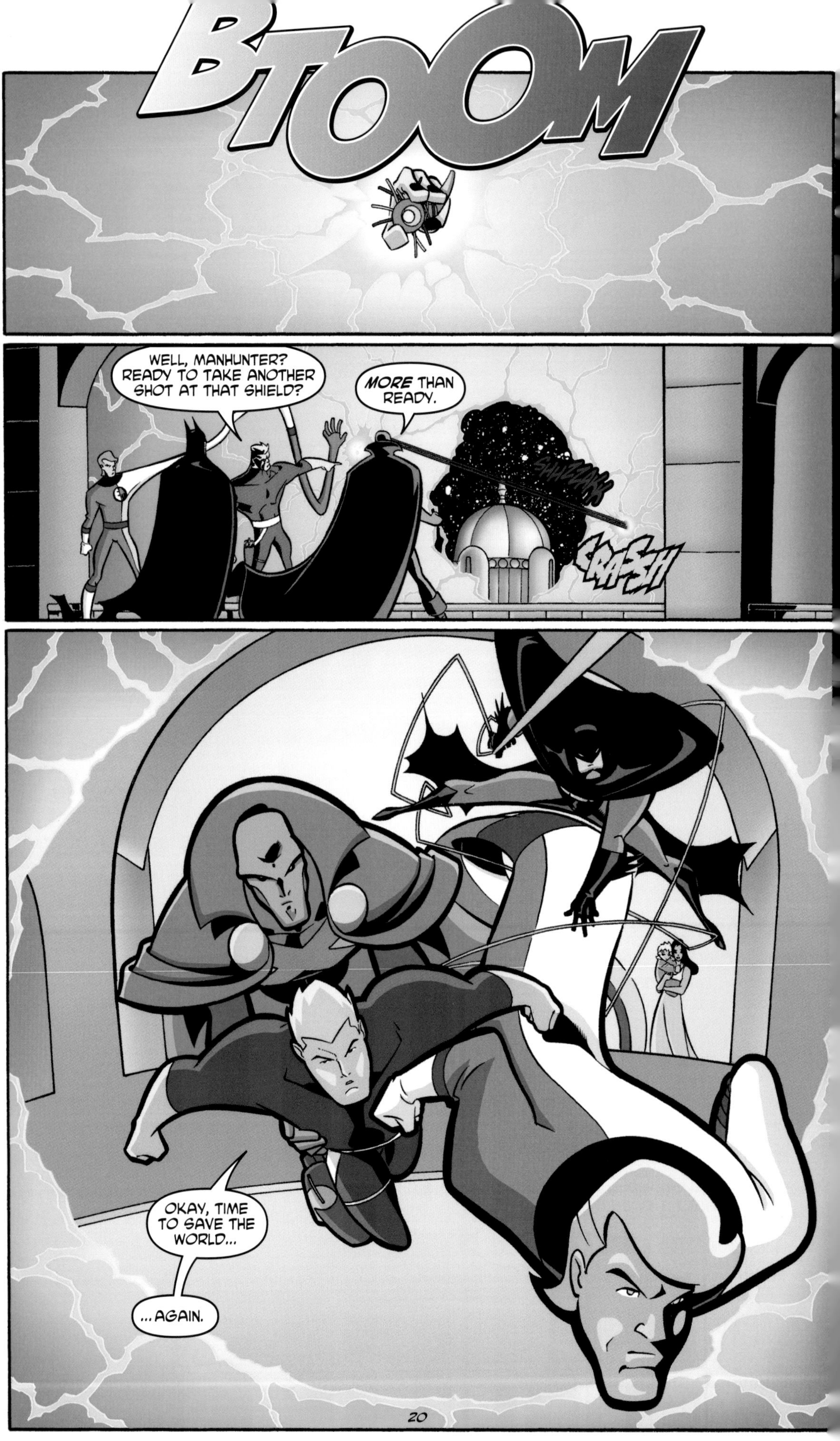
BTOOM
WELL, MANHUNTER? READY TO TAKE ANOTHER SHOT AT THAT SHIELD?
MORE THAN READY.
SHHZZAKK
CRASSH
OKAY, TIME TO SAVE THE WORLD...
...AGAIN.

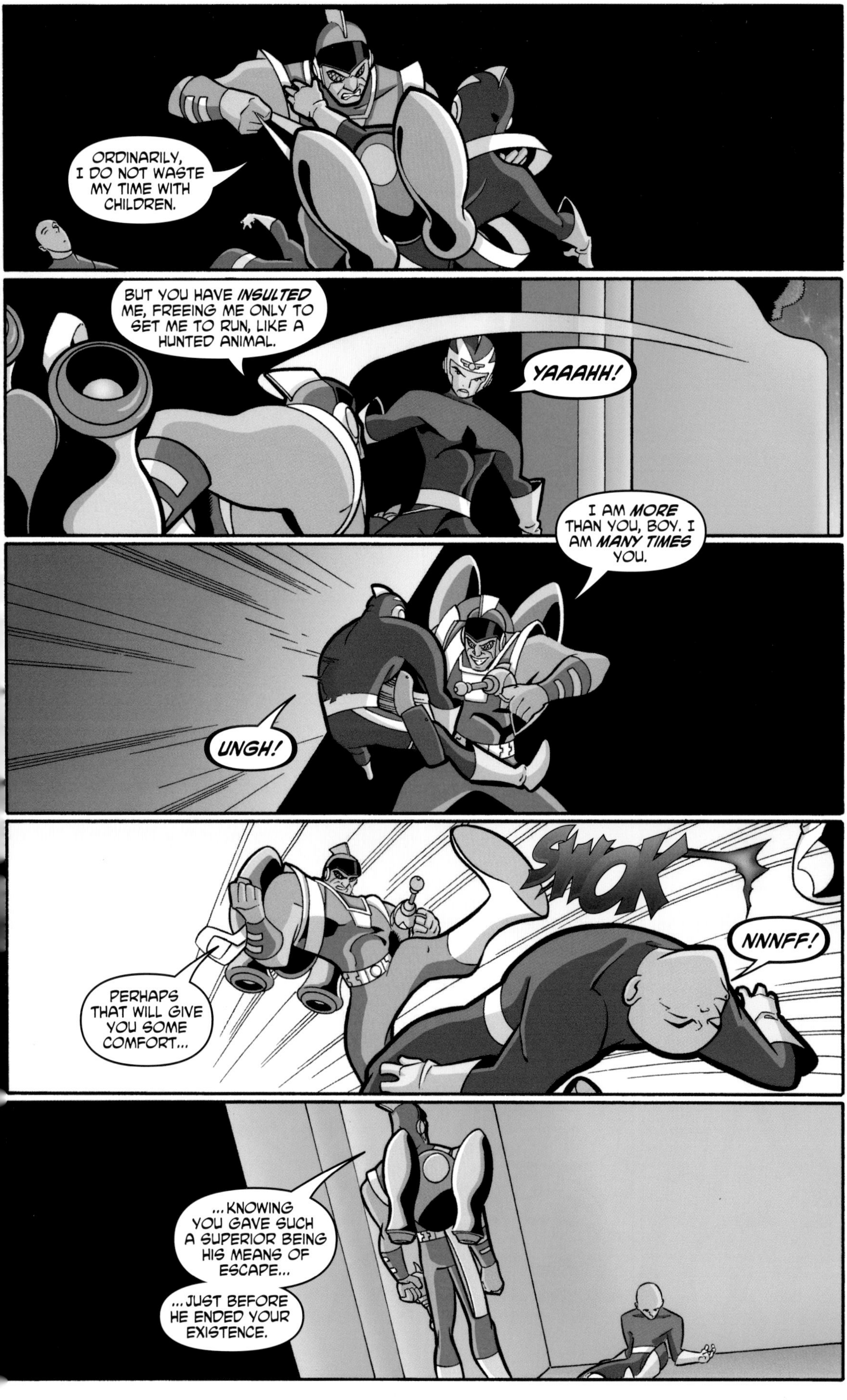
ORDINARILY, I DO NOT WASTE MY TIME WITH CHILDREN.
BUT YOU HAVE *INSULTED* ME, FREEING ME ONLY TO SET ME TO RUN, LIKE A HUNTED ANIMAL.
YAAAHH!
I AM *MORE* THAN YOU, BOY. I AM *MANY TIMES* YOU.
UNGH!
SMOK
NNNFF!
PERHAPS THAT WILL GIVE YOU SOME COMFORT...
...KNOWING YOU GAVE SUCH A SUPERIOR BEING HIS MEANS OF ESCAPE...
...JUST BEFORE HE ENDED YOUR EXISTENCE.

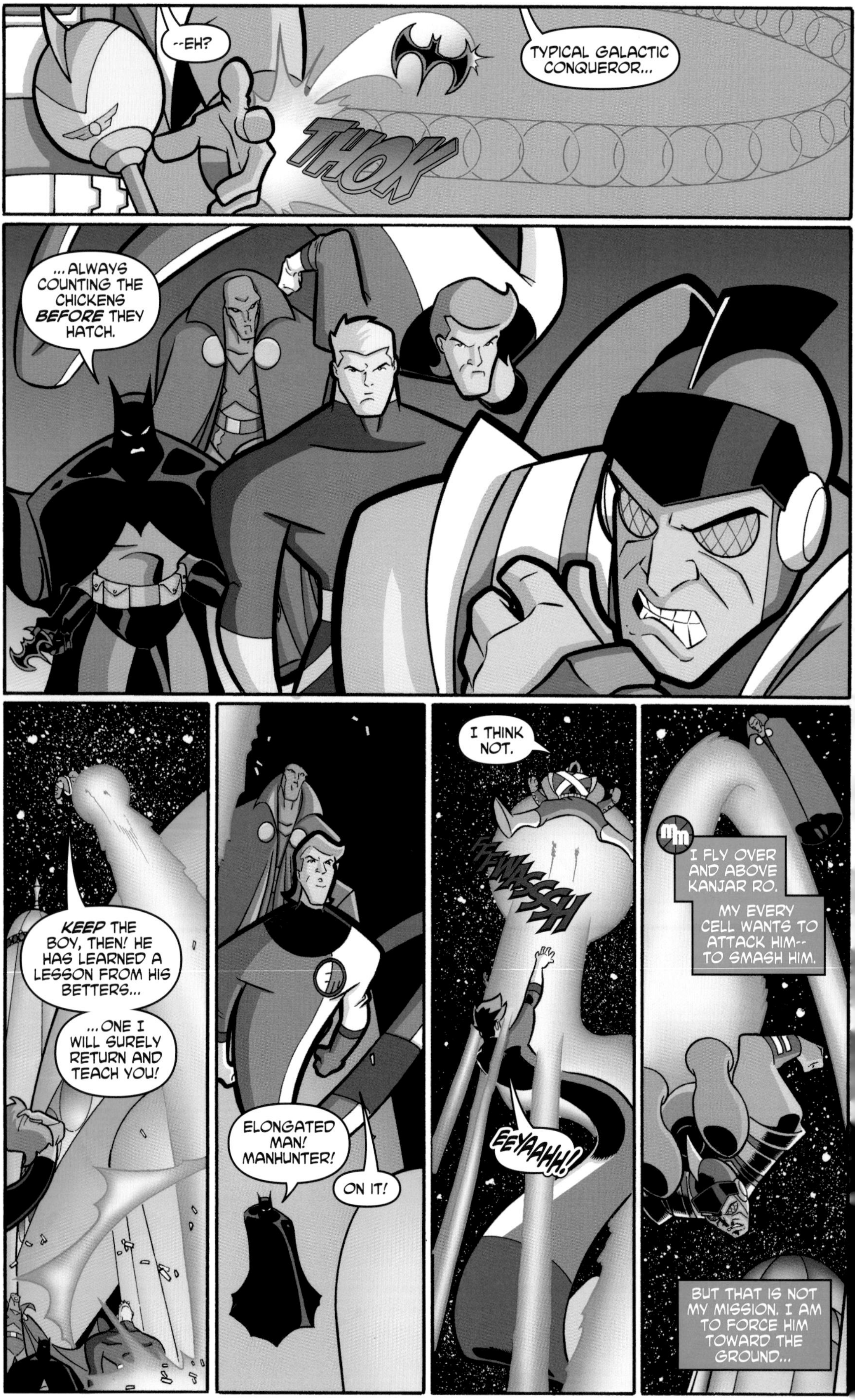
--EH?
TYPICAL GALACTIC CONQUEROR...
THOK
...ALWAYS COUNTING THE CHICKENS *BEFORE* THEY HATCH.
KEEP THE BOY, THEN! HE HAS LEARNED A LESSON FROM HIS BETTERS...
...ONE I WILL SURELY RETURN AND TEACH YOU!
ELONGATED MAN! MANHUNTER!
ON IT!
I THINK NOT.
FFFWASSSH
EEYAAHH!
I FLY OVER AND ABOVE KANJAR RO.
MY EVERY CELL WANTS TO ATTACK HIM-- TO SMASH HIM.
BUT THAT IS NOT MY MISSION. I AM TO FORCE HIM TOWARD THE GROUND...

...SO WE MAY DEAL WITH HIM IN NUMBERS.

AAAK!

NICELY DONE, MANHUNTER.

HE'LL BE EASY PICKINGS ONCE WE REMOVE HIS JET PACK...!

I SEE WE ARE MUCH *ALIKE,* EARTHMAN...

...COUNTING BEFORE THE *HATCHING!*

MANHUNTER, LOOK--

THWRMM

NNGGH!

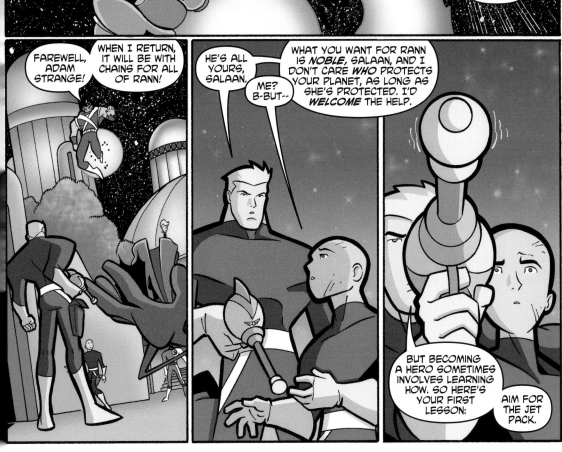

FAREWELL, ADAM STRANGE!

WHEN I RETURN, IT WILL BE WITH CHAINS FOR ALL OF RANN!

HE'S ALL YOURS, SALAAN.

ME? B-BUT--

WHAT YOU WANT FOR RANN IS *NOBLE,* SALAAN, AND I DON'T CARE *WHO* PROTECTS YOUR PLANET, AS LONG AS SHE'S PROTECTED. I'D *WELCOME* THE HELP.

BUT BECOMING A HERO SOMETIMES INVOLVES LEARNING HOW. SO HERE'S YOUR FIRST LESSON:

AIM FOR THE JET PACK.

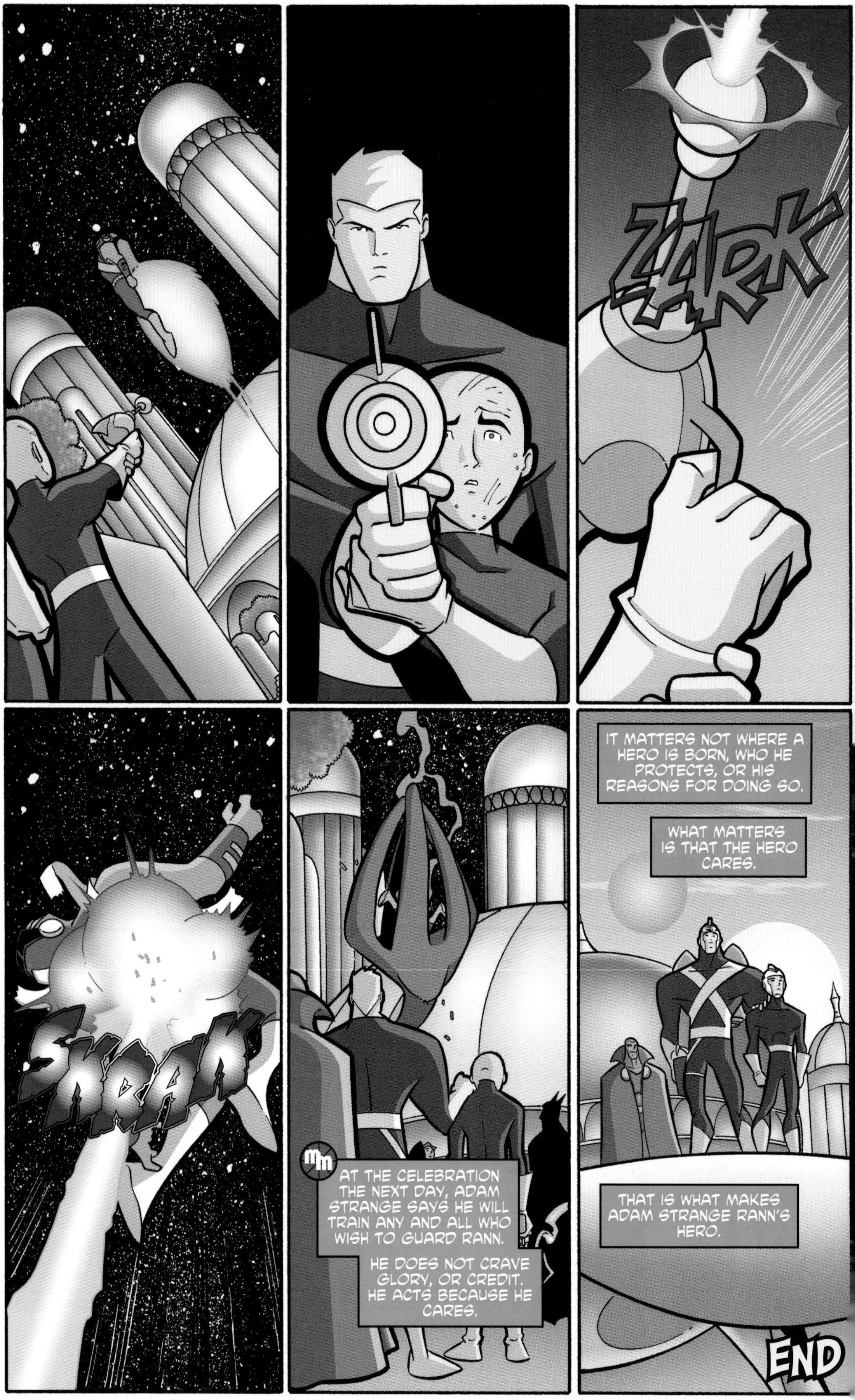
ZARK
SKRAK
AT THE CELEBRATION THE NEXT DAY, ADAM STRANGE SAYS HE WILL TRAIN ANY AND ALL WHO WISH TO GUARD RANN.
HE DOES NOT CRAVE GLORY, OR CREDIT. HE ACTS BECAUSE HE CARES.
IT MATTERS NOT WHERE A HERO IS BORN, WHO HE PROTECTS, OR HIS REASONS FOR DOING SO.
WHAT MATTERS IS THAT THE HERO CARES.
THAT IS WHAT MAKES ADAM STRANGE RANN'S HERO.
END

JUSTICE LEAGUE
UNLIMITED

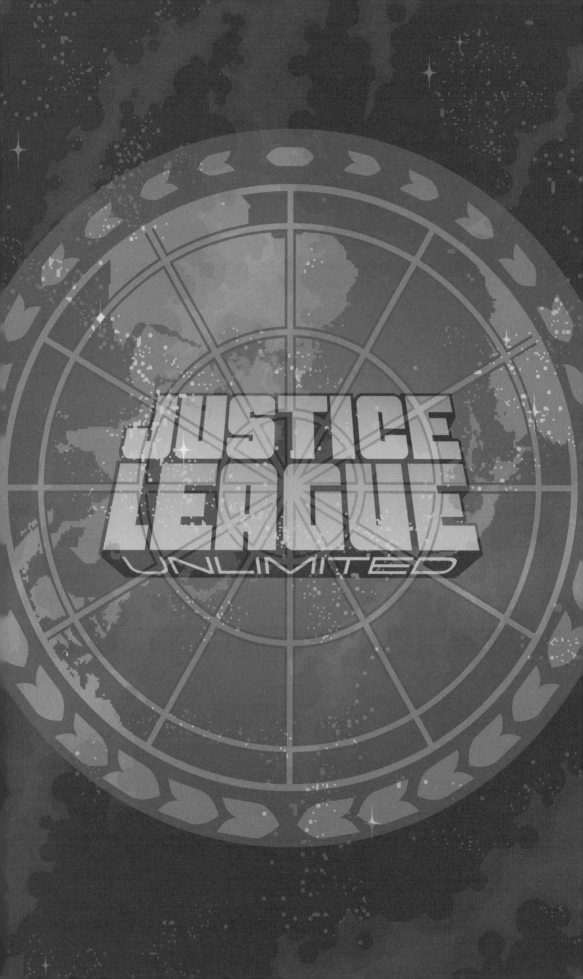

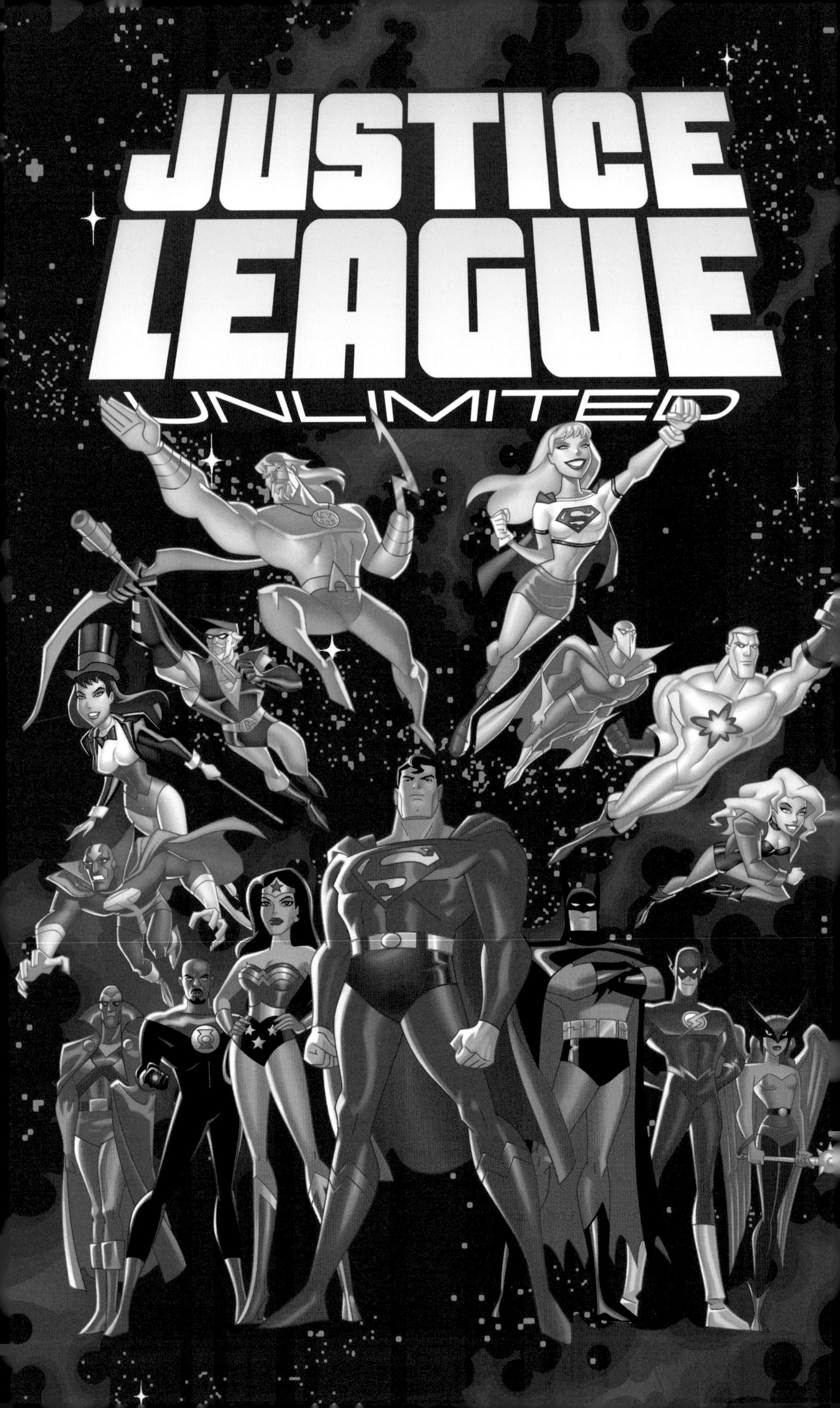
JUSTICE LEAGUE
UNLIMITED

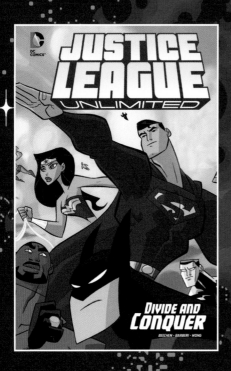

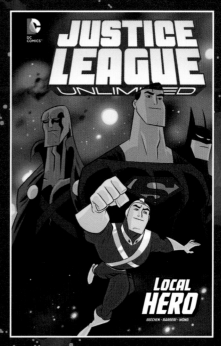

DC COMICS
JUSTICE LEAGUE
UNLIMITED
DIVIDE AND CONQUER
BEECHEN · BARBERI · WONG

DC COMICS
JUSTICE LEAGUE
UNLIMITED
POKER FACE
BEECHEN · BEAVERS

DC COMICS
JUSTICE LEAGUE
UNLIMITED
SMALL TIME
BEECHEN · BARBERI · WONG

DC COMICS
JUSTICE LEAGUE
UNLIMITED
LOCAL HERO
BEECHEN · BARBERI · WONG

CREATORS

ADAM BEECHEN WRITER

Adam Beechen has written a variety of TV cartoons, including *Ben Ten: Alien Force*, *Teen Titans*, *Batman: The Brave and the Bold*, *The Batman* (for which he received an Emmy nomination), *Rugrats*, *The Wild Thornberrys*, *X-Men: Evolution*, and *Static Shock*, as well as the live-action series *Ned's Declassified School Survival Guide* and *The Famous Jett Jackson*. He is also the author of *Hench*, a graphic novel, and has scripted many comic books, including *Batgirl*, *Teen Titans*, *Robin*, and *Justice League Unlimited*. In addition Adam has written dozens of children's books, as well as an original young adult novel, *What I Did On My Hypergalactic Interstellar Summer Vacation*.

CARLO BARBERI PENCILLER

Carlo Barberi is a professional comic book artist from Monterrey, Mexico. His best-known works for DC Comics include *Batman: The Brave and the Bold*, *The Flash*, *Blue Beetle*, *Gen 13*, and *Justice League Unlimited*.

WALDEN WONG INKER

Walden Wong is a professional comic book artist, inker, and colorist. He's worked on some of DC Comics' top characters, including Superman, Batman, Wonder Woman, and more.

WORD GLOSSARY

citizens (SIT-i-zuhn)--members of a city, state, or country

commission (kuh-MISH-uhn)--in use or ready for use

conqueror (KONG-kur-ur)--one who takes or gains something by force of arms

embrace (em-BRAYSS)--to take up readily or gladly

existence (eg-ZIST-stenss)--the fact or the state of having been real, or of being real

Kryptonite (KRIP-tuh-nite)--a radioactive material from the planet Krypton, able to weaken the superpowers of Superman and Supergirl

menace (MEN-iss)--someone or something that represents a threat

radiation (ray-dee-AY-shuhn)--energy radiated in the form of waves or particles

tendencies (TEN-duhn-seez)--leanings toward a particular kind of thought or action

J.L.U. GLOSSARY

KRYPTONITE

A radioactive material from the planet Krypton, able to weaken the superpowers of Superman, a member of the Justice League.

MARTIAN VISION

Martian Manhunter is gifted with "Martian Vision," a superpower that allows this hero to see through walls and fire heat vision beams from his eyes.

STRETCHABILITY

Elongated Man, a member of the Justice League, can stretch and shape his body into a variety of different forms.

VISUAL QUESTIONS & PROMPTS

1. In the panel at right [from page 11], what do you think the young boy, Salaad, feels about Adam Strange? How did you come to your conclusion?

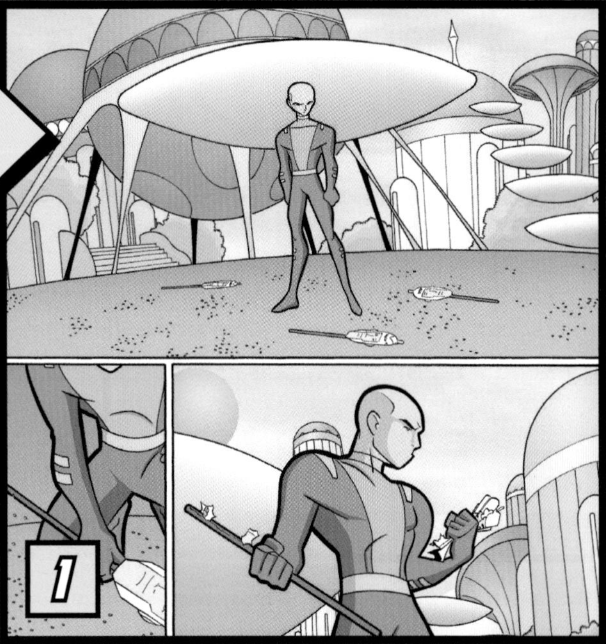

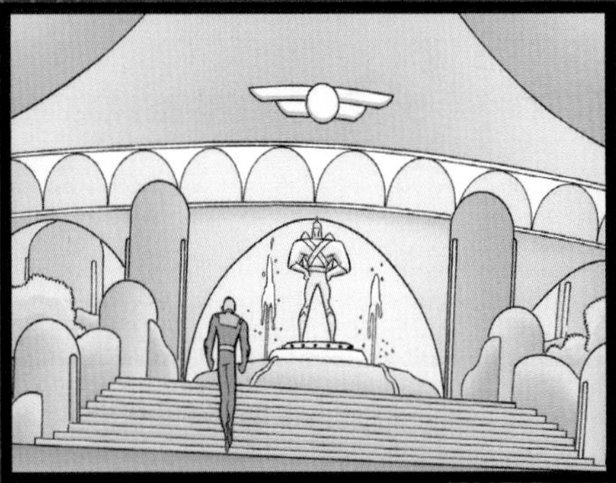

2. In comic books, sound effects [also known as SFX] are used to show sounds, such as an explosion. Make a list of all the sound effects in this book, and then write a definition for each term. Soon, you'll have your own SFX dictionary!

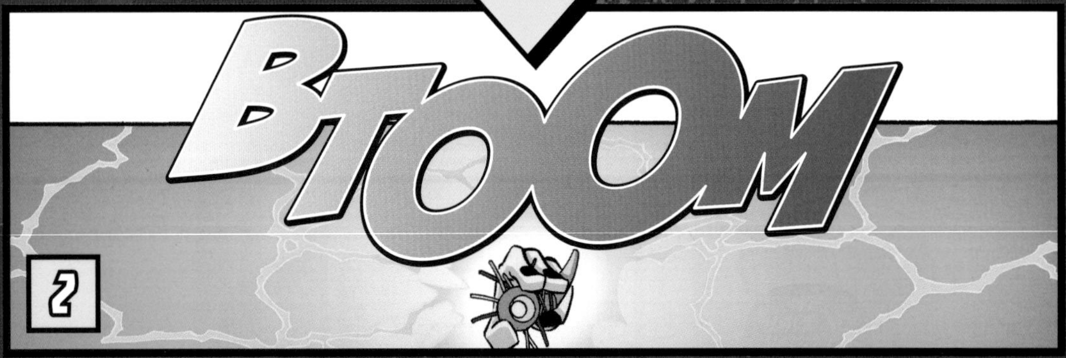
BTOOM

3. What is happening to Martian Manhunter in the panel at right [from page 16]? Explain your answer using clues from the story.

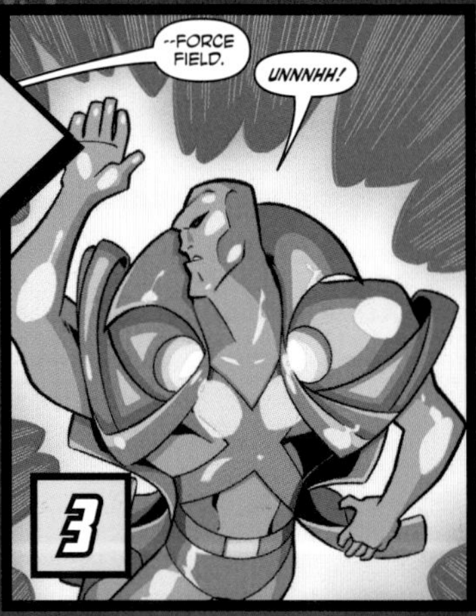
--FORCE FIELD.
UNNNHH!

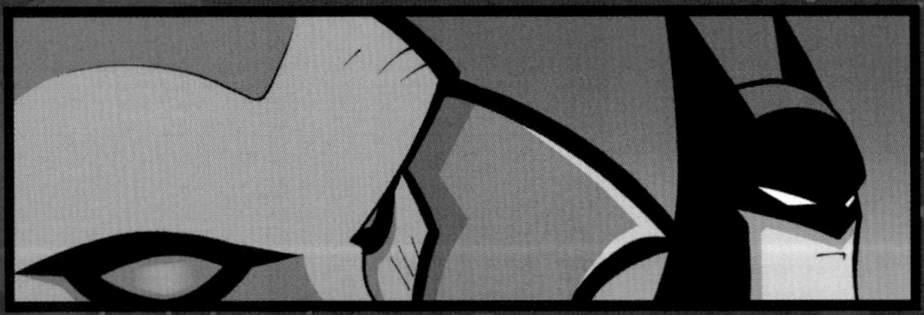

4. At the end of this story, do you think Adam Strange has forgiven Salaad for his mistakes? If so, why?

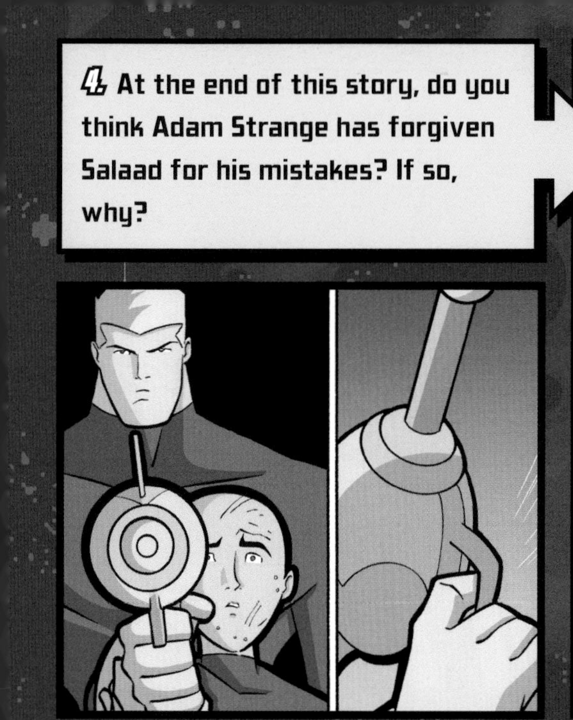

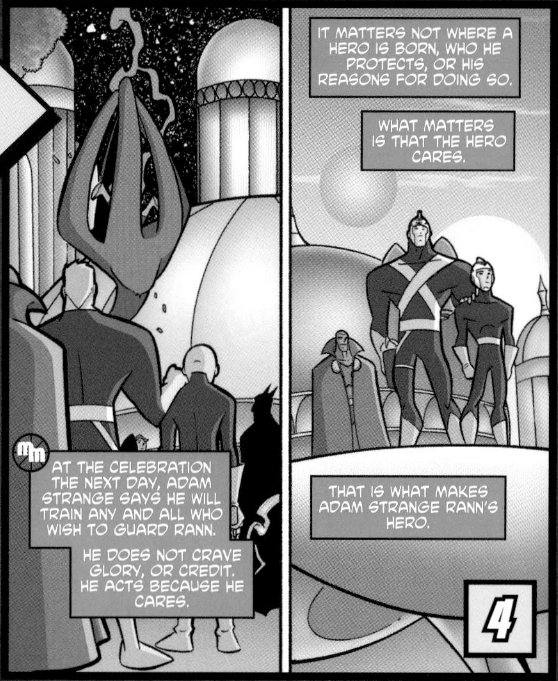
AT THE CELEBRATION THE NEXT DAY, ADAM STRANGE SAYS HE WILL TRAIN ANY AND ALL WHO WISH TO GUARD RANN.
HE DOES NOT CRAVE GLORY, OR CREDIT. HE ACTS BECAUSE HE CARES.
IT MATTERS NOT WHERE A HERO IS BORN, WHO HE PROTECTS, OR HIS REASONS FOR DOING SO.
WHAT MATTERS IS THAT THE HERO CARES.
THAT IS WHAT MAKES ADAM STRANGE RANN'S HERO.
4

5. Super heroes have many different powers. In the panel below [from page 21], which super heroes do you think have the power of flight? How are the others able to sore through the air?

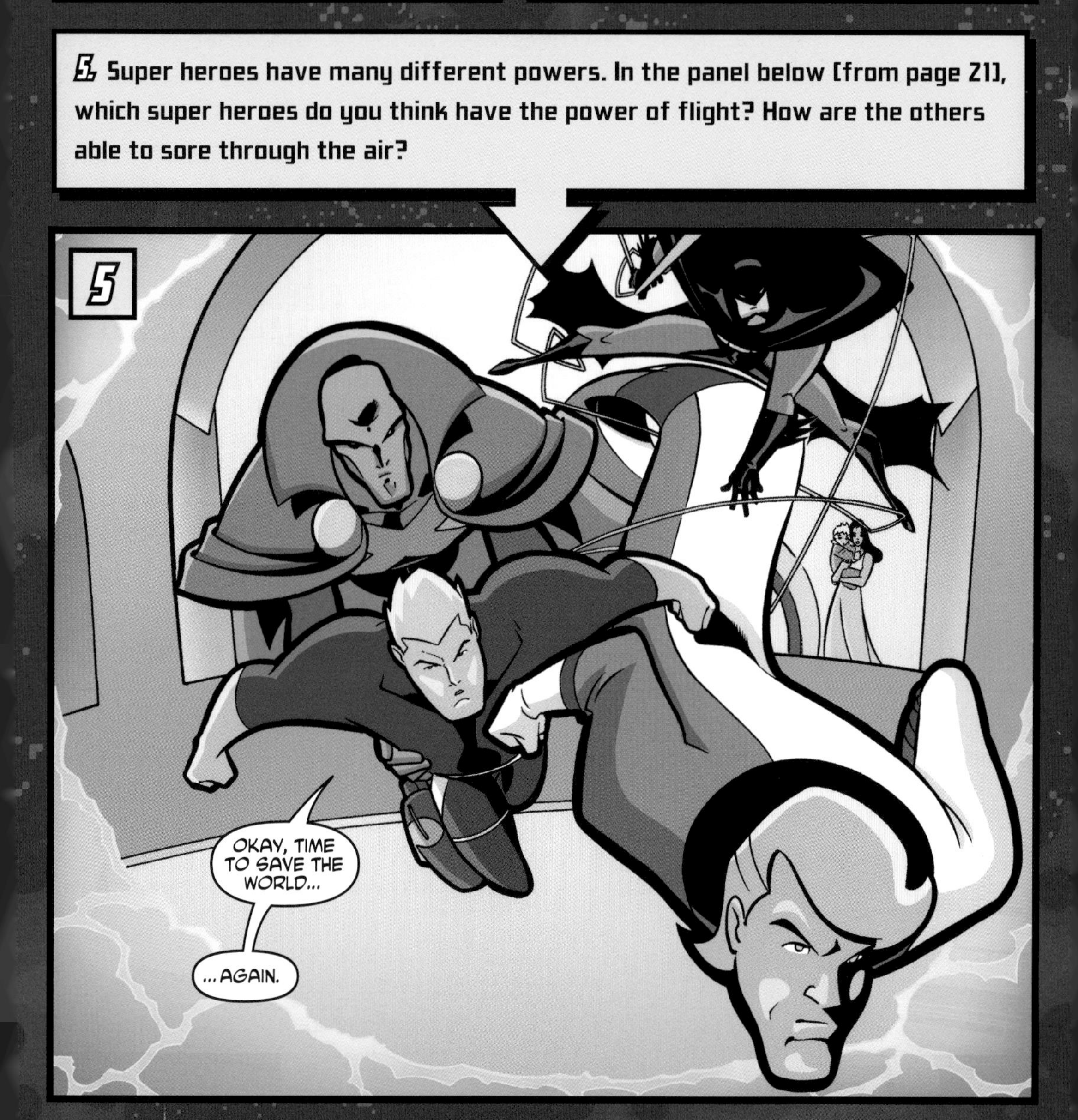
5
OKAY, TIME TO SAVE THE WORLD...
...AGAIN.

WANT EVEN MORE?

GO TO...

WWW.*CAPSTONEKIDS*.com

Then find cool websites and more books
like this one at *www.facthound.com*.

Just type in the BOOK ID:
9781434247162